THE GREY ROOM

The Grey Room

Eden Phillpotts

MYSTERIOUSPRESS.COM

INTEGRATED MEDIA
NEW YORK

Originally published in 1922.

Cover design by Amanda Shaffer.

ISBN: 978-1-5040-9397-2

This edition published in 2024 by MysteriousPress.com/Open Road Integrated Media, Inc.
180 Maiden Lane
New York, NY 10038
www.openroadmedia.com

INTRODUCTION

Puzzle: Multiple victims are murdered by an unknown agent while alone in a locked room despite being warned that it was haunted.

A guest at a house party is curious to hear the history of the bedroom in the huge old Tudor mansion that appears to be cursed. A woman a dozen years previously had died in it of an unknown cause that defied the most thorough analysis that great medical minds could bring to the problem. She had been alone in the room, which was found to be locked on the inside when she failed to respond to calls. The room, although a beautiful one with lovely views, was then superstitiously sealed and thereafter used mainly for storage.

After-dinner conversations about ghosts and supernatural doings, interspersed with reminders of God and reason, convince one of the young visitors to sleep overnight in the so-called haunted room against the wishes of his host. He stealthily prepares himself to spend an uneventful night's slumber but is found dead in the morning.

The police are called and a thorough search for clues to the cause of death fails to reach a satisfactory conclusion. Various guests and members of the household are interviewed in an attempt to find a suspect or a viable motive—also without success.

And still more deaths follow.

Members of the great old family talk a great deal about the hereafter, speculating about God and ghosts, reality and superstition, and are generally sanguine about the remarkable occurrences unfolding as fear and uncertainty hover above their heads. When another person dies, there are stiff upper lips to spare. "To die is no hardship for the dead, remember," one of them comfortingly tells the young woman who has just been made a widow.

In spite of the fact that *The Grey Room* is, admittedly, sometimes long-winded, it is nonetheless a compelling mystery, unsolved until its very end, and regarded highly enough to be selected by Howard Haycraft and Ellery Queen for their "Definitive Library of Detective-Crime-Mystery Fiction."

Published in 1921, it is one of more than seventy mystery novels and short story collections written by the evidently indefatigable Phillpotts, which are among the only of his books to be published in the United States.

Perhaps the best known is *The Red Redmaynes* (1922), which involves the efforts of a snuff-taking American detective, Peter Ganns, to solve a case concerning the calculated extermination of an entire family.

Phillpotts also wrote several mystery novels using the pseudonym Harrington Hext, including *The Thing at Their Heels* (1923), in which a radical clergyman is the villain, and *Who Killed Cock Robin?* (1924, published in England as *Who Killed Diana?*), in which even the victim's identity is questionable. Cock Robin and Jenny Wren are nicknames for twin daughters of an English archdeacon.

For aficionados of short stories, Phillpotts' greatest

accomplishment was his first work, *My Adventure in the Flying Scotsman: A Romance of London and North-Western Railway Shares* (1988), published individually in a slim volume that is extremely rare and sought after by collectors. Ellery Queen thought so highly of it that he selected it for his *Queen's Quorum*, his list of the one hundred six greatest volumes of mystery stories.

Regardless of his prolific output as a mystery writer, many would argue that his greatest contribution to the genre was his well-publicized encouragement of a youthful Agatha Christie, with his ongoing assistance being instrumental in her subsequent development.

Born in Mount Aboo, India, in 1862, Phillpotts spent most of his life in England, mainly in Devon. He studied acting at the age of seventeen but did not stay with it for very long, saying, "I abandoned the art on finding my ability did not justify perseverance." He took a job with an insurance company, staying for ten years, while writing stories and poems in his spare time before resigning to devote full time to writing. He married in 1892 and, when his wife died in 1928, remarried the next year. He had a son and a daughter, Adelaide, a novelist with whom he collaborated on several plays.

Over the course of a long life (he did not die until he reached ninety-eight in 1960), he wrote more than one hundred and fifty volumes, the most important of which are undoubtedly his long series of Dartmoor novels, which have frequently been compared to Thomas Hardy's Wessex novels.

—Otto Penzler
New York, January 2023

THE GREY ROOM

CHAPTER I.

THE HOUSE PARTY

The piers of the main entrance of Chadlands were of red brick, and upon each reposed a mighty sphere of grey granite. Behind them stretched away the park, where forest trees, nearly shorn of their leaves at the edge of winter, still answered the setting sun with fires of thinning foliage. They sank away through stretches of brake fern, and already amid their trunks arose a thin, blue haze—breath of earth made visible by coming cold. There was frost in the air, and the sickle of a new moon hung where dusk of evening dimmed the green of the western sky.

The guns were returning, and eight men with three women arrived at the lofty gates. One of the party rode a grey pony, and a woman walked on each side of him. They chattered together, and the little company of tweed-clad people passed into Chadlands Park and trudged forward, where the manor house rose half a mile ahead.

Then an old man emerged from a lodge, hidden behind a grove of laurel and bay within the entrance, and shut the great gates of scroll iron. They were of a flamboyant Italian period, and more arrestive than distinguished. Panelled upon them, and belonging to a later day than they, had been imposed two iron coats of arms, with crest above and motto beneath—the heraldic bearings of the present owner of Chadlands. He set store upon such things, but was not responsible for the work. A survival himself, and steeped in ancient opinions, his coat, won in a forgotten age, interested him only less than his Mutiny medal—his sole personal claim to public honor. He had served in youth as a soldier, but was still a subaltern when his father died and he came into his kingdom.

Now, Sir Walter Lennox, fifth baronet, had grown old, and his invincible kindness of heart, his archaic principles, his great wealth, and the limited experiences of reality, for which such wealth was responsible, left him a popular and respected man. Yet he aroused much exasperation in local landowners from his generosity and scorn of all economic principles; and while his tenants held him the very exemplar of a landlord, and his servants worshipped him for the best possible reasons, his friends, weary of remonstrance, were forced to forgive his bad precedents and a mistaken liberality quite beyond the power of the average unfortunate who lives by his land. But he managed his great manor in his own lavish way, and marvelled that other men declared difficulties with problems he so readily solved. That night, after a little music, the Chadlands' house party drifted to the billiard-room, and while most of the men, after a heavy day far afield, were content to lounge by a great open hearth where a wood fire burned, Sir Walter, who had been on a pony most of the time, declared himself unwearied, and demanded a game.

"No excuses, Henry," he said; and turned to a young man lounging in an easy-chair outside the fireside circle.

The youth started. His eyes had been fixed on a woman sitting beside the fire, with her hand in a man's. It was such an attitude as sophisticated lovers would only assume in private but the pair were not sophisticated and lovers still, though married. They lacked self-consciousness, and the husband liked to feel his wife's hand in his. After all, a thing impossible until you are married may be quite seemly afterwards, and none of their amiable elders regarded their devotion with cynicism.

"All right, uncle!" said Henry Lennox.

He rose—a big fellow with heavy shoulders, a clean-shaven, youthful face, and flaxen hair. He had been handsome, save for a nose with a broken bridge, but his pale brown eyes were fine, and his firm mouth and chin well modelled. Imagination and reflection marked his countenance.

Sir Walter claimed thirty points on his scoring board, and gave a miss with the spot ball.

"I win to-night," he said.

He was a small, very upright man, with a face that seemed to belong to his generation, and an expression seldom to be seen on a man younger than seventy. Life had not puzzled him; his moderate intellect had taken it as he found it, and, through the magic glasses of good health, good temper, and great wealth, judged existence a desirable thing and quite easy to conduct with credit. "You only want patience and a brain," he always declared. Sir Walter wore an eyeglass. He was growing bald, but preserved a pair of grey whiskers still of respectable size. His face, indeed, belied him, for it was moulded in a stern pattern. One had guessed him a martinet until his amiable opinions and easy-going personality were manifested. The old man was not vain; he knew that a world very different from his own extended round about him. But he was puzzle-headed, and had never been shaken from his life-long complacency by circumstances.

EDEN PHILLPOTTS

He had been disappointed in love as a young man, and only married late in life. He had no son, and was a widower—facts that, to his mind, quite dwarfed his good fortune in every other respect. He held the comfortable doctrine that things are always levelled up, and he honestly believed that he had suffered as much sorrow and disappointment as any Lennox in the history of the race.

His only child and her cousin, Henry Lennox, had been brought up together and were of an age—both now twenty-six. The lad was his uncle's heir, and would succeed to Chadlands and the title; and it had been Sir Walter's hope that he and Mary might marry. Nor had the youth any objection to such a plan. Indeed, he loved Mary well enough; there was even thought to be a tacit understanding between them, and they grew up in a friendship which gradually became ardent on the man's part, though it never ripened upon hers. But she knew that her father keenly desired this marriage, and supposed that it would happen some day.

They were, however, not betrothed when the war burst upon Europe, and Henry, then one-and-twenty, went from the Officers' Training Corps to the Fifth Devons, while his cousin became attached to the Red Cross and nursed at Plymouth. The accident terminated their shadowy romance and brought real love into the woman's life, while the man found his hopes at an end. He was drafted to Mesopotamia, speedily fell sick of jaundice, was invalided to India, and, on returning to the front, saw service against the Turks. But chance willed that he won no distinction. He did his duty under dreary circumstances, while to his hatred of war was added the weight of his loss when he heard that Mary had fallen in love. He was an ingenuous, kindly youth—a typical Lennox, who had developed an accomplishment at Harrow and suffered for it by getting his nose broken when winning the heavy-weight championship of the public schools in his nineteenth year. In the East he still boxed, and after his love story was ended, the epidemic of poetry-making took Henry also, and he wrote a volume of harmless verse, to the undying amazement of his family.

For Mary Lennox the war had brought a sailor husband. Captain Thomas May, wounded rather severely at Jutland, lost his heart to the plain but attractive young woman with a fine figure who nursed him back to strength, and, as he vowed, had saved his life. He was an impulsive man of thirty, brown-bearded, black-eyed, and hot-tempered. He came from a little Somerset vicarage and was the only son of a clergyman, the Rev. Septimus May. Knowing the lady as "Nurse Mary" only, and falling passionately in love for the first time in his life, he proposed on the day he was allowed to sit up, and since Mary Lennox shared his emotions, also for the first time, he was accepted before he even knew her name.

It is impossible to describe the force of love's advent for Mary Lennox. She had come to believe herself as vaguely committed to her cousin, and imagined that her affection for Henry amounted to as much as she was ever likely to feel for a man. But reality awakened her, and its glory did not make her selfish, since her nature was not constructed so to be; it only taught her what love meant, and convinced her that she could never marry anybody on earth but the stricken sailor. And this she knew long before he was well enough to give a sign that he even appreciated her ministry. The very whisper of his voice sent a thrill through her before he had gained strength to speak aloud. And his deep tones, when she heard them, were like no voice that had fallen on her ear till then. The first thing that indicated restoring health was his request that his beard might be trimmed; and he was making love to her three days after he had been declared out of danger. Then did Mary begin to live, and looking back, she marvelled how horses and dogs and a fishing-rod had been her life till now. The revelation bewildered her and she wrote her emotions in many long pages to her cousin. The causes of such changes she did not indeed specify, but he read between the lines, and knew it was a man and not the war that had so altered and deepened her outlook. He had never done it, and he could not be angry with her now, for she had pretended no ardor of emotion to him. Young though he was, he always feared that she liked him not after the way of a lover. He had hoped to open her eyes some day, but it was given to another to do so.

He felt no surprise, therefore, when news of her engagement reached him from herself. He wrote the letter of his life in reply, and was at pains to laugh at their boy-and-girl attachment, and lessen any regret she might feel on his account. Her father took it somewhat hardly at first, for he held that more than sufficient misfortunes, to correct the balance of prosperity in his favor, had already befallen him. But he was deeply attached to his daughter, and her magical change under the new and radiant revelation convinced him that she had now awakened to an emotional fulness of life which could only be the outward sign of love. That she was in love for the first time also seemed clear; but he would not give his consent until he had seen her lover and heard all there was to know about him. That, however, did not alarm Mary, for she believed that Thomas May must prove a spirit after Sir Walter's heart. And so he did. The sailor was a gentleman; he had proposed without the faintest notion to whom he offered his penniless hand, and when he did find out, was so bewildered that Mary assured her father she thought he would change his mind.

"If I had not threatened him with disgrace and breach of promise, I do think he would have thrown me over," she said.

And now they had been wedded for six months, and Mary sat by the great log fire with her hand in Tom's. The sailor was on leave, but expected to return to his ship at Plymouth in a day or two. Then his father-in-law had promised to visit the great cruiser, for the Navy was a service of which he knew little. Lennoxes had all been soldiers or clergymen since a great lawyer founded the race.

The game of billiards proceeded, and Henry caught his uncle in the eighties and ran out with an unfinished fifteen. Then Ernest Travers and his wife—old and dear friends of Sir Walter—played a hundred up, the lady receiving half the game. Mr. Travers was a Suffolk man, and had fagged for Sir Walter at Eton. Their comradeship had lasted a lifetime, and no year passed without reciprocal visits. Travers also looked at life with the eyes of a wealthy man. He was sixty-five, pompous, large, and rubicund—a "backwoodsman" of a pattern obsolescent. His wife, ten years younger than himself, loved pleasure, but she had done more than her duty, in her opinion, and borne him two sons and a daughter. They were colorless, kind-hearted people who lived in a circle of others like themselves. The war had sobered them, and at an early stage robbed them of their younger boy.

Nelly Travers won her game amid congratulations, and Tom May challenged another woman, a Diana, who lived for sport and had joined the house party with her uncle, Mr. Felix Fayre-Michell. But Millicent Fayre-Michell refused.

"I've shot six partridges, a hare, and two pheasants to-day," said the girl, "and I'm half asleep."

Other men were present also of a type not dissimilar. It was a conventional gathering of rich nobodies, each a big frog in his own little puddle, none known far beyond it and none with sufficient intellect or ability to create for himself any position in the world save that won by the accident of money made by their progenitors.

Had it been necessary for any of them to earn his living, only in some very modest capacity and on a very modest plane might they have done so. Of the entire company only one—the youngest—could claim even the celebrity that attached to his little volume of war verses.

And now upon the lives of these every-day folk was destined to break an event unique and extraordinary. Existence, that had meandered without personal incident save of a description common to them all, was, within twelve hours, to confront men and women alike with reality. They were destined to endure at close quarters an occurrence so astounding and unparalleled that, for once in their lives, they would find themselves interesting to the wider world beyond their own limited circuit, and, for their friends and acquaintance, the centre of a nine days' wonder.

Most of them, indeed, merely touched the hem of the mystery and were not involved therein, but even for them a reflected glory shone. They were at least objects of attraction elsewhere, and for many months furnished conversation of a more interesting and exciting character than any could ever claim to have provided before.

The attitude to such an event, and the opinions concerning it, of such people might have been pretty accurately predicted; nor would it be fair to laugh at their terror and bewilderment, their confusion of tongues and the fatuous theories they adventured by way of explanation. For wiser than they—men experienced in the problems of humanity and trained to solve its enigmas— were presently in no better case.

A very trivial and innocent remark was prelude to the disaster; and had the speaker guessed what his jest must presently mean in terms of human misery, grief, and horror, it is certain enough that he would not have spoken.

The women were gone to bed and the men sat around the fire smoking and admiring Sir Walter's ancient blend of whisky. He himself had just flung away the stump of his cigar and was admonishing his son-in-law. "Church to-morrow, Tom. None of your larks. When first you came to see me, remember, you went to church twice on Sunday like a lamb. I'll have no backsliding."

"Mary will see to that, governor."

"And you, Henry."

Sir Walter, disappointed of his hopes respecting his nephew and daughter, had none the less treated the young man with tact and tenderness. He felt for Henry; he was also fond of him and doubted not that the youth would prove a worthy successor. Thomas May was one with whom none could quarrel, and he and his wife's old flame were now, after the acquaintance of a week, on friendly terms.

"I shan't fail, uncle."

"Will anybody have another whisky?" asked Sir Walter, rising.

It was the signal for departure and invariably followed the stroke of a deep-mouthed, grandfather clock in the hall. When eleven sounded, the master rose; but to-night he was delayed. Tom May spoke.

"Fayre-Michell has never heard the ghost story, governor," he said, "and Mr. Travers badly wants another drink. If he doesn't have one, he won't sleep all night. He's done ten men's work to-day."

Mr. Fayre-Michell spoke.

"I didn't know you had a ghost, Sir Walter. I'm tremendously interested in psychical research and so on. If it's not bothering you and keeping you up—"

"A ghost at Chadlands, Walter?" asked Ernest Travers. "You never told me."

"Ghosts are all humbug," declared another speaker—a youthful "colonel" of the war.

"I deprecate that attitude, Vane. It may certainly be that our ghost is a humbug, or, rather, that we have no such thing as a ghost at all. And that is my own impression. But an idle generality is always futile—indeed, any generality usually is. You have, at least, no right to say, 'Ghosts are all humbug.' Because you cannot prove they are. The weight of evidence is very much on the other side."

"Sorry," said Colonel Vane, a man without pride. "I didn't know you believed in 'em, Sir Walter."

"Most emphatically I believe in them."

"So do I," declared Ernest Travers. "Nay, so does my wife— for the best possible reason. A friend of hers actually saw one."

Mr. Fayre-Michell spoke.

"Spiritualism and spirits are two quite different things," he said. "One may discredit the whole business of spiritualism and yet firmly believe in spirits."

He was a narrow-headed, clean-shaven man with grey hair and moustache. He had a small body on very long legs, and though a veteran now, was still one of the best game shots in the West of England.

Ernest Travers agreed with him. Indeed, they all agreed. Sir Walter himself summed up.

"If you're a Christian, you must believe in the spirits of the dead," he declared; "but to go out of your way to summon these spirits, to call them from the next world back to ours, and to consult people who profess to be able to do so— extremely doubtful characters, as a rule—that I think is much to be condemned. I deny that there are any living mediums of communication between the spirit world and this one, and I should always judge the man or woman who claimed such power to be a charlatan. But that spirits of the departed have appeared and been recognized by the living, who shall deny?

"My son-in-law has a striking case in his own recent experience. He actually knows a man who was going to sail on the Lusitania, and his greatest friend on earth, a soldier who fell on the Maine, appeared to him and advised him not to do so. Tom's acquaintance could not say that he heard words uttered, but he certainly recognized his dead friend as he stood by his bedside, and he received into his mind a clear warning before the vision disappeared. Is that so, Tom?"

"Exactly so, sir. And Jack Thwaites—that was the name of the man in New York—told four others about it, and three took his tip and didn't sail. The fourth went; but he wasn't drowned. He came out all right."

"The departed are certainly proved to appear in their own ghostly persons—nay, they often have been seen to do so," admitted Travers. "But I will never believe they are at our beck and call, to bang tambourines or move furniture. We cannot ring up the dead as we ring up the living on a telephone. The idea is insufferable and indecent. Neither can anybody be used as a mouth-piece in that way, or tell us the present position or occupation and interests of a dead man—or what he smokes, or how his liquor tastes. Such ideas degrade our impressions of life beyond the grave. They are, if I may say so, disgustingly anthropomorphic. How can we even take it for granted that our spirits will retain a human form and human attributes after death?"

"It would be both weak-minded and irreligious to attempt to get at these things, no doubt," declared Colonel Vane.

"And they make confusion worse confounded by saying that

evil spirits pretend sometimes to hoodwink us by posing as good spirits. Now, that's going too far," said Henry Lennox.

"But your own ghost, Sir Walter?" asked Fayre-Michell. "It is a curious fact that most really ancient houses have some such addition. Is it a family spectre? Is it fairly well authenticated? Does it reign in a particular spot of house or garden? I ask from no idle curiosity. It is a very interesting subject if approached in a proper spirit, as the Psychical Research Society, of which I am a member, does approach it."

"I am unprepared to admit that we have a ghost at all," repeated Sir Walter. "Ancient houses, as you say, often get some legend tacked on to them, and here a garden walk, or there a room, or passage, is associated with something uncanny and contrary to experience. This is an old Tudor place, and has been tinkered and altered in successive generations. We have one room at the eastern end of the great corridor which always suffered from a bad reputation. Nobody has ever seen anything in our time, and neither my father nor grandfather ever handed down any story of a personal experience. It is a bedroom, which you shall see, if you care to do so. One very unfortunate and melancholy thing happened in it. That was some twelve years ago, when Mary was still a child—two years after my dear wife died."

"Tell us nothing that can cause you any pain, Walter," said Ernest Travers.

"It caused me very acute pain at the time. Now it is old history and mercifully one can look back with nothing but regret. One must, however, mention an incident in my father's time, though it has nothing to do with my own painful experience. However, that is part of the story—if story it can be called. A death occurred in the Grey Room when I was a child. Owing to the general vague feeling entertained against it, we never put guests there, and so long ago as my father's day it was relegated to a store place and lumber-store. But one Christmas, when we were very full, there came quite unexpectedly on Christmas Eve an aunt of my father—an extraordinary old character who never did anything that might be foreseen. She had never come to the family reunion before, yet appeared on this occasion, and declared that, as this was going to be her last Christmas on earth, she had felt it right to join the clan— my father being the head of the family. Her sudden advent strained our resources, I suppose, but she herself reminded us of the Grey Room, and, on hearing that it was empty, insisted on occupying it. The place is a bedroom, and my father, who personally entertained no dislike or dread of it, raised not the least objection to the strong-minded old lady's proposal. She retired, and was found dead on Christmas morning. She had not gone to bed, but was just about to do so, apparently, when she had fallen down and died. She was eighty-eight, had undergone a lengthy coach journey from Exeter, and had eaten a remarkably good dinner before going to bed. Her maid was not suspected, and the doctor held her end in no way unusual. It was certainly never associated with anything but natural causes. Indeed, only events of much later date served to remind me of the matter. Then one remembered the spoiled Christmas festivities and the callous and selfish anger of myself and various other young people that our rejoicings should be spoiled and Christmas shorn of all its usual delights.

"But twelve years ago Mary fell ill of pneumonia— dangerously—and a nurse had to be summoned in haste, since her own faithful attendant, Jane Bond, who is still with us, could not attend her both day and night. A telegram to the Nurses' Institute brought Mrs. Gilbert Forrester—'Nurse Forrester,' as she preferred to be called. She was a little bit of a thing, but most attractive and capable. She had been a nurse before she married a young medical man, and upon his unfortunate death she returned to her profession. She desired her bedroom to be as near the patient as possible, and objected, when she found it arranged at the other end of the corridor. 'Why not the next room?' she inquired; and I had to tell her that the next room suffered from a bad name and was not used. 'A bad name—is it unwholesome?' she asked; and I explained that traditions credited it with a sinister influence. 'In fact,' I said, 'it is supposed to be haunted. Not,' I added, 'that anything has ever been seen, or heard in my lifetime; but nervous people do not like that sort of room, and I should never take the responsibility of putting anybody into it without telling them.' She laughed. 'I'm not in the least afraid of ghosts, Sir Walter,' she said, 'and that must obviously be my room, if you please. It is necessary I should be as near my patient as possible, so that I can be called at once if her own nurse is anxious when I am not on duty.'

"Well, we saw, of course, that she was perfectly right. She was a fearless little woman, and chaffed Masters and the maids while they lighted a fire and made the room comfortable. As a matter of fact, it is an exceedingly pleasant room in every respect. Yet I hesitated, and could not say that I was easy about it. I felt conscious of a discomfort which even her indifference did not entirely banish. I attributed it to my acute anxiety over Mary—also to a shadow of—what? It may have been irritation at Nurse Forrester's unconcealed contempt for my superstition. The Grey Room is large and commodious with a rather fine oriel window above our eastern porch. She was delighted, and rated me very amusingly for my doubts. 'I hope you'll never call such a lovely room haunted again after I have gone,' said she.

"Mary took to her, and really seemed easier after she had been in the sick-room an hour. She loved young people, and had an art to win them. She was also a most accomplished and quick-witted nurse. There seemed to be quite a touch of genius about her. Her voice was melodious and her touch gentle. I could appreciate her skill, for I was never far from my daughter's side during that anxious day. Mrs. Forrester came at the critical hours, but declared herself very sanguine from the first.

"Night fell; the child was sleeping and Jane Bond arrived to relieve the other about ten o'clock. Then the lady retired, directed that she should be called at seven o'clock, or at any moment sooner, if Jane wanted her. I sat with Jane I remember until two, and then turned in myself. Before I did so, Mary drank some milk and seemed to be holding her strength well. I was worn out, and despite my anxiety fell into deep sleep, and did not wake until my man called me half an hour earlier than usual. What he told me brought me quickly to my senses and out of bed. Nurse Forrester had been called at seven o'clock, but had not responded. Nor could the maid open the door, for it was locked. A quarter of an hour later the housekeeper and Jane Bond had loudly summoned her without receiving any reply. Then they called me.

"I could only direct that the door should be forced open as speedily as possible, and we were engaged in this task when Mannering, my medical man, who shot with us to-day, arrived to see Mary. I told him what had happened. He went in to look at my girl, and felt satisfied that she was holding her own well—indeed, he thought her stronger; and just as he told me so the door into the Grey Room yielded. Mannering and my house-keeper, Mrs. Forbes, entered the room, while Masters, Fred Caunter, my footman, who had broken down the lock, and I remained outside.

"The doctor presently called me, and I went in. Nurse Forrester was apparently lying awake in bed, but she was not awake. She slept the sleep of death. Her eyes were open, but

17

glazed, and she was already cold. Mannering declared that she had been dead for a good many hours. Yet, save for a slight but hardly unnatural pallor, not a trace of death marked the poor little creature. An expression of wonder seemed to sit on her features, but otherwise she was looking much as I had last seen her, when she said 'Good-night.' Everything appeared to be orderly in the room. It was now flooded with the first light of a sunny morning, for she had drawn her blind up and thrown her window wide open. The poor lady passed out of life without a sound or signal to indicate trouble, for in the silence of night Jane Bond must have heard any alarm had she raised one. To me it seemed impossible to believe that we gazed upon a corpse. But so it was, though, as a matter of form, the doctor took certain measures to restore her. But animation was not suspended; it had passed beyond recall.

"There was held a post-mortem examination, and an inquest, of course; and Mannering, who felt deep professional interest, asked a friend from Plymouth to conduct the examination. Their report astounded all concerned and crowned the mystery, for not a trace of any physical trouble could be discovered to explain Nurse Forrester's death. She was thin, but organically sound in every particular, nor could the slightest trace of poison be reported. Life had simply left her without any physical reason. Search proved that she had brought no drugs or any sort of physic with her, and no information to cast the least light came from the institution for which she worked. She was a favorite there, and the news of her sudden death brought sorrow to her many personal friends.

"The physicians felt their failure to find a natural and scientific cause for her death. Indeed, Dr. Mordred, from Plymouth, an eminent pathologist, trembled not a little about it, as Mannering afterwards told me. The finite mind of science hates, apparently, to be faced with any mystery beyond its power to explain. It regards such an incident as a challenge to human intellect, and does not remember that we are encompassed with mystery as with a garment, and that every day and every night are laden with phenomena for which man cannot account, and never will.

"Nurse Forrester's relations—a sister and an old mother—came to the funeral. Also her dearest woman friend, another professional nurse, whose name I do not recollect. She was buried at Chadlands, and her grave lies near our graves. Mary loves to tend it still, though to her the dead woman is but a name. Yet to this day she declares that she can remember Nurse Forrester's voice through her fever—gentle, yet musical and cheerful. As for me, I never mourned so brief an acquaintance so heartily. To part with the bright creature, so full of life and kindliness, and to stand beside her corpse but eight or nine hours afterwards, was a chastening and sad experience."

Sir Walter became pensive, and did not proceed for the space of a minute. None, however, spoke until he had again done so:

"That is the story of what is called our haunted room, so far as this generation is concerned. What grounds for its sinister reputation existed in the far past I know not—only a vague, oral tradition came to my father from his, and it is certain that neither of them attached any personal importance to it. But after such a peculiar and unfortunate tragedy, you will not be surprised that I regarded the chamber as ruled out from my domiciliary scheme, and denied it to any future guests."

"Do you really associate the lady's death with the room, Walter?" asked Mr. Travers.

"Honestly I do not, Ernest. And for this reason: I deny that any malignant, spiritual personality would ever be permitted by the Creator to exercise physical powers over the living, or destroy human beings without reason or justice. The horror of such a possibility to the normal mind is sufficient argument against it. Causes beyond our apparent knowledge were responsible for the death of Nurse Forrester; but who shall presume to say that was really so? Why imagine anything so irregular? I prefer to think that had the post-mortem been conducted by somebody else, subtle reasons for her death might have appeared. Science is fallible, and even specialists make outrageous mistakes."

"You believe she died from natural causes beyond the skill of those particular surgeons to discover?" asked Colonel Vane.

"That is my opinion. Needless to say, I should not tell Mannering so. But to what other conclusion can a reasonable man come? I do not, of course, deny the supernatural, but it is weak-minded to fall back upon it as the line of least resistance."

Then Fayre-Michell repeated his question. He had listened with intense interest to the story.

"Would you deny that ghosts, so to call them, can be associated with one particular spot, to the discomfort and even loss of reason, or life, of those that may be in that spot at the psychological moment, Sir Walter?"

"Emphatically I would deny it," declared the elder. "However tragic the circumstances that might have befallen an unfortunate being in life at any particular place, it is, in my opinion, monstrous to suppose his disembodied spirit will hereafter be associated with the place. We must be reasonable, Felix. Shall the God Who gave us reason be Himself unreasonable?"

"And yet there are authentic—However, I admit the weight of your argument."

"At the same time," ventured Mr. Travers, "none can deny that many strange and terrible things happen, from hidden causes quite beyond human power to explain."

"They do, Ernest; and so I lock up my Grey Room and rule it out of our scheme of existence. At present it is full of lumber—old furniture and a pack of rubbishy family portraits that only deserve to be burned, but will some day be restored, I suppose."

"Not on my account, Uncle Walter," said Henry Lennox. "I have no more respect for them than yourself. They are hopeless as art."

"No, no one must restore them. The art is I believe very bad, as you say, but they were most worthy people, and this is the sole memorial remaining of them."

"Do let us see the room, governor," urged Tom May. "Mary showed it to me the first time I came here, and I thought it about the jolliest spot in the house."

"So it is, Tom," said Henry. "Mary says it should be called the Rose Room, not the grey one."

"All who care to do so can see it," answered Sir Walter, rising. "We will look in on our way to bed. Get the key from my key-cabinet in the study, Henry. It's labelled 'Grey Room.'"

CHAPTER II.

AN EXPERIMENT

Ernest Travers, Felix Fayre-Michell, Tom May, and Colonel Vane followed Sir Walter upstairs to a great corridor, which ran the length of the main front, and upon which opened a dozen bedrooms and dressing-rooms. They proceeded to the eastern extremity. It was lighted throughout, and now their leader took off an electric bulb from a sconce on the wall outside the room they had come to visit.

"There is none in there," he explained, "though the light was installed in the Grey Room as elsewhere when I started my own plant twenty years ago. My father never would have it. He disliked it exceedingly, and believed it aged the eyes."

Henry arrived with the key. The door was unlocked, and the light established. The party entered a large and lofty chamber with ceiling of elaborate plaster work and silver-grey walls, the paper on which was somewhat tarnished. A pattern of dim, pink roses as large as cabbages ran riot over it. A great oriel window looked east, while a smaller one opened upon the south. Round the curve of the oriel ran a cushioned seat eighteen inches above the ground, while on the western side of the room, set in the internal wall, was a modern fireplace with a white Adams mantel above it. Some old, carved chairs stood round the walls, and in one corner, stacked together, lay half a dozen old oil portraits, grimy and faded. They called for the restorer, but were doubtfully worth his labors. Two large chests of drawers, with rounded bellies, and a very beautiful washing-stand also occupied places round the room, and against the inner wall rose a single, fourposter bed of Spanish chestnut, also carved. A grey, self-colored carpet covered the floor, and on one of the chests stood a miniature bronze copy of the Faun of Praxiteles.

The apartment was bright and cheerful of aspect. Nothing gloomy or depressing marked it, nor a suggestion of the sinister.

"Could one wish for a more amiable looking room?" asked Fayre-Michell.

They gazed round them, and Ernest Travers expressed admiration at the old furniture.

"My dear Walter, why hide these things here?" he asked. "They are beautiful, and may be valuable, too."

"I've been asked the same question before," answered the owner. "And they are valuable. Lord Bolsover offered me a thousand guineas for those two chairs; but the things are heirlooms in a sort of way, and I shouldn't feel justified in parting with them. My grandfather was furniture mad—spent half his time collecting old stuff on the Continent. Spain was his happy hunting ground."

"It's positively a shame to doom these chairs to a haunted room, uncle," declared Henry.

But the other shook his head and smothered a yawn.

"The house is too full as it is." he said.

"Mary wants you to scrap dozens of things," replied his nephew. "Then there'd be plenty of room."

"You'll do what you please when your turn comes, and no doubt cast out my tusks and antlers and tiger-skins, which I know you don't admire. Wait in patience, Henry. And we will now go to bed," answered the elder. "I am fatigued, and it must be nearly midnight."

Then Tom May brought their thoughts back to the reason of the visit.

"Look here, governor," he said. "It's a scandal to give a champion room like this a bad name and shut it up. You've fallen into the habit, but you know it's all nonsense. Mary loves this room. I'll make you a sporting offer. Let me sleep in it to-night, and then, when I report a clean bill to-morrow, you can throw it open again and announce it is forgiven without a stain on its character. You've just said you don't believe spooks have the power to hurt anybody. Then let me turn in here."

Sir Walter, however, refused.

"No, Tom; most certainly not. It's far too late to go over the ground again and explain why, but I don't wish it."

"A milder-mannered room was never seen," said Ernest Travers. "You must let me look at it by daylight, and bring Nelly. The ceiling, too, is evidently very fine—finer even than the one in my room."

"The ceilings here were all the work of Italians in Tudor times," explained his friend. "They are Elizabethan. The plaster is certainly wonderful, and my ceilings are considered as good as anything in the country, I believe."

He turned, and the rest followed him.

Henry removed the electric bulb, and restored it to its place outside. Then his uncle gave him the key.

"Put it back in the cabinet," he said. "I won't go down again."

The party broke up, and all save Lennox and the sailor went to their rooms. The two younger men descended together and, when out of ear-shot of his uncle, Henry spoke.

"Look here, Tom," he said, "you've given me a tip. I'm going to camp out in the Grey Room to-night. Then, in the morning, I'll tell Uncle Walter I have done so, and the ghost's number will be up."

"Quite all right, old man—only the plan must be modified. I'll sleep there. I'm death on it, and the brilliant inspiration was mine, remember."

"You can't. He refused to let you."

"I didn't hear him."

"Oh, yes, you did—everybody did. Besides, this is fairly my task—you won't deny that. Chadlands will be mine, some day, so it's up to me to knock this musty yarn on the head once and for all. Could anything be more absurd than shutting up a fine room like that? I'm really rather ashamed of Uncle Walter."

"Of course it's absurd but, honestly, I'm rather keen about this. I'd dearly love to add a medieval phantom to my experiences, and only wish I thought anything would show up. I beg you'll raise no objection. It was my idea, and I very much wish to make the experiment. Of course, I don't believe in anything supernatural."

They went back to the billiard-room, dismissed Fred Caunter, the footman, who was waiting to put out the lights, and continued their discussion. The argument began to grow strenuous, for each proved determined, and who owned the stronger will seemed a doubtful question.

For a time, since no conclusion could satisfy both, they abandoned the centre of contention and debated, as their elders had done, on the general question. Henry declared himself not wholly convinced. He adopted an agnostic attitude, while Tom frankly disbelieved. The one preserved an open mind, the other scoffed at apparitions in general.

"It's humbug to say sailors are superstitious now," he asserted. "They might have been, but my experience is that they are no more credulous than other people in these days. Anyway, I'm not. Life is a matter of chemistry. There's no mumbo jumbo about it, in my opinion. Chemical analysis has reached down to hormones and enzymes and all manner of subtle secretions discovered by this generation of inquirers; but it's all organic. Nobody has ever found anything that isn't. Existence depends on matter, and when the chemical process breaks down, the organism perishes and leaves nothing. When a man can't go on breathing, he's dead, and there's an end of him."

But Henry had read modern science also.

"What about the vital spark, then? Biologists don't turn down the theory of vitalism, do they?"

"Most of them do, who count, my dear chap. The presence of a vital spark—a spark that cannot be put out—is merely a theory with nothing to prove it. When he dies, the animating principle doesn't leave a man, and go off on its own. It dies too. It was part of the man—as much as his heart or brain."

"That's only an opinion. Nobody can be positive. We don't know anything about what life really means, and we haven't got the machinery to find out."

"By analogy we can," argued Tom. "Where are you going to draw the line? Life is life, and a sponge is just as much alive as a herring; a nettle is just as much alive as an oak-tree; and an oak-tree is just as much alive as you are. What becomes of its vital spark when you eat an oyster?"

"You wouldn't believe in a life after death at all, then?"

"It's a pure assumption, Henry. I'd like to believe in it—who wouldn't? Because, if you honestly did, it would transform this life into something infinitely different from what it is."

"It ought to—yet it doesn't seem to."

"It ought to, certainly. If you believe this life is only the portal to another of much greater importance, then—well, there you are. Nothing matters but trying to make everybody else believe it, too. But as a matter of fact, the people who do believe it, or think they do, seem to me just as concentrated on this life and just as much out to get the very best they can from it, and wring it dry, as I am, who reckon it's all."

"They believe as a matter of course, and don't seem to realize how much their belief ought to imply," confessed Henry.

"Why do they believe? Because most of them haven't really thought about it more than a turnip thinks. They dwell in a foggy sort of way on the future life when they go to church on Sundays; then they return home and forget all about it till next Sunday."

Lennox brought him back to the present difference.

"Well, seeing you laugh at ghosts, and I remain doubtful, it's only fair that I sleep in the Grey Room. You must see that. Ghosts hate people who don't believe in them. They'd cold shoulder you; but in my case they might feel I was good material, worth convincing. They might show up for me in a friendly spirit. If they show for you, it will probably be to bully you."

Tom laughed.

"That's what I want. I'd like to have it out and talk sense to a spook, and show him what an ass he's making of himself. The governor was right about that. When Fayre-Michell asked if he believed in them loafing about a place where they'd been murdered or otherwise maltreated, he rejected the idea."

"Yet a woman certainly died there, and without a shadow of reason."

"She probably died for a very good reason, only we don't happen to know it."

Henry tried a different argument.

"You're married, and you matter; I'm not married, and don't matter to anybody."

"Humbug!"

"Mary wouldn't like it, anyway; you know that."

"True—she'd hate it. But she won't know anything about it till to-morrow. She always sleeps in her old nursery when she comes here, and I'm down the corridor at the far end. She'd have a fit if she knew I'd turned in next door to her and was snoozing in the Grey Room; but she won't know till I tell her of my rash act to-morrow. Don't think I'm a fool. Nobody loves life better than I do, and nobody has better reason to. But I'm positive that this is all rank nonsense, and so are you really. We know there's nothing in the room with a shadow of supernatural danger about it. Besides, you wouldn't want to sleep there so badly if you believed anything wicked was waiting for you. You're tons cleverer than I am—so you must agree about that."

Lennox was bound to confess that he entertained no personal fear. They still argued, and the clock struck midnight. Then the sailor made a suggestion.

"Since you're so infernally obstinate, I'll do this. We'll toss up, and the winner can have the fun. That's fair to both."

The other agreed; he tossed a coin, and May called "tails," and won.

He was jubilant, while Henry showed a measure of annoyance. The other consoled him.

"It's better so, old man. You're highly strung and nervy, and a poet and all that sort of thing. I'm no better than a prize ox, and don't know what nerves mean. I can sleep anywhere, anyhow. If you can sleep in a submarine, you bet you can in a nice, airy

Elizabethan room, even if it is haunted. But it's not; that's the whole point. There's not a haunted room in the world. Get me your service revolver, like a good chap."

Henry was silent, and Tom rose to make ready for his vigil.

"I'm dog-tired, anyhow," he said. "Nothing less than Queen Elizabeth herself will keep me awake, if it does appear."

Then the other surprised him.

"Don't think I want to go back on it. You've won the right to make the experiment—if we ignore Uncle Walter. But—well, you'll laugh, yet, on my honor, Tom, I've got a feeling I'd rather you didn't. It isn't nerves. I'm not nervy any more than you are. I'm not suggesting that I go now, of course. But I do ask you to think better of it and chuck the thing."

"Why?"

"Well, one can't help one's feelings. I do feel a rum sort of conviction at the bottom of my mind that it's not good enough. I can't explain; there are no words for it that I know, but it's growing on me. Intuition, perhaps."

"Intuition of what?"

"I can't tell you. But I ask you not to go."

"You were going if you'd won the toss?"

"I know."

"Then your growing intuition is only because I won it. Hanged if I don't think you want to funk me, old man!"

"I couldn't do that. But it's different me going and you going. I've got nothing to live for. Don't think I'm maudlin, or any rot of that sort; but you know all about the past. I've never mentioned it to you, and, of course, you haven't to me; and I never should have. But I will now. I loved Mary with all my heart and soul, Tom. She didn't know how much, and probably I didn't either. But that's done, and no man on earth rejoices in her great happiness more than I do. And no man on earth is going to be a better or a truer friend to you and her than, please God, I shall be. But that being so, can't you see the rest? My life ended in a way when the dream of my life ended. I attach no importance to living for itself, and if anything final happened to me it wouldn't leave a blank anywhere. You're different. In sober honesty you oughtn't to run into any needless danger—real or imaginary. I'm thinking of Mary only when I say that—not you."

"But I deny the danger."

"Yes; only you might listen. So did I, but I deny it no longer. The case is altered when I tell you in all seriousness—when I take my oath if you like—that I do believe now there is something in this. I don't say it's supernatural, and I don't say it isn't; but I do feel deeply impressed in my mind now, and it's growing stronger every minute, that there's something here out of the common and really infernally dangerous."

The other looked at him in astonishment.

"What bee has got into your bonnet?"

"Don't call it that. It's a conviction, Tom. Do be guided by me, old chap!"

The sailor flushed a little, emptied his glass, and rose.

"If you really wanted to choke me off, you chose a funny way to do so. Surely it only needed this to determine anybody. If you, as a sane person, honestly believe there's a pinch of danger in that blessed place, then I certainly sleep there to-night, or else wake there."

"Let me come, too, then, Tom."

"That be damned for a yarn! Ghosts don't show up for two people—haven't got pluck enough. If I get any sport, I'll be quite straight about it, and you shall try your luck to-morrow."

"I can only make it a favor; and not for your own sake, either."

"I know. Mary will be sleeping the sleep of the just in the next room. How little she'll guess! Perhaps, if I see an apparition worthy of the Golden Age, I'll call her up."

"Do oblige me, May."

"In anything on earth but this thing. It's really too late now. Don't you see you've defeated your own object? You mustn't ask me to throw up the sponge to your sudden intuition of danger sprung on me at the eleventh hour. I won the toss, and can't take my orders from you, old chap, can I?"

The other, in his turn, grew a little warm.

"All right. I've spoken. I think you're rather a fool to be so obstinate. It isn't as if a nervous old woman was talking to you. But you'll go your own way. It doesn't matter a button to me, and I only made it a favor for somebody else's sake."

"We'll leave it at that, then. May I trouble you for the key? And your revolver, too. I haven't got mine here."

Henry hesitated. The key was in the pocket of his jacket.

"It is a matter of honor, Lennox," said the sailor.

The other handed over the key on this speech, and prepared to go.

"I'll get the revolver," he said.

"Thanks. Look me up in the morning, if you're awake first," added May; but the other did not answer.

He let Tom precede him, and then turned out the lights. Other lights he also extinguished as they left the hall and ascended the stairs. The younger's pride was struggling for mastery; but he conquered it and spoke again.

"I wish to Heaven you could see it from another point of view than your own, Tom."

"I have no point of view. You're rather exasperating, and don't seem to understand that, even if I might have changed my mind before, it's impossible now."

31

"That's really only a foolish sort of pride. If I chose my words clumsily—"

"You did. The devil and all his angels wouldn't make me climb down now."

The younger left him, and returned in a minute or two with the revolver.

"Good-night," he said.

"Good-night, old boy. Thank you. Loaded?"

"In all the chambers. Funny you should want it."

"Take it back, then."

But Henry did not answer, and they parted. Each sought his own bedroom, and while Lennox retired at once and might have been expected to pass a night more mentally peaceful than the other, in reality it was not so.

The younger slept ill, while May suffered no emotion but annoyance. He was contemptuous of Henry. It seemed to him that he had taken a rather mean and unsporting line, nor did he believe for a moment that he was honest. Lennox had a modern mind; he had been through the furnace of war; he had received a first-class education. It seemed impossible to imagine that he spoke the truth, or that his sudden suspicion of real perils, beyond human power to combat, could be anything but a spiteful attempt to put May off, after he himself had lost the toss. Yet that seemed unlike a gentleman. Then the allusion to Mary perturbed the sailor. He could not quarrel with the words, but he resented the advice, seeing what it was based upon.

His anger lessened swiftly, however, and before he started his adventure he had dismissed Henry from his mind. He put on pyjamas and a dressing-gown, took a candle, a railway-rug, his watch, and the loaded revolver.

Then he walked quietly down the corridor to the Grey Room. On reaching it his usual good temper returned, and he found himself entirely happy and contented. He unlocked the forbidden entrance, set his candle by the bed, and locked the door again from inside. He rolled up his dressing-gown for a pillow, and placed his watch and revolver and candle at his hand on a chair. A few broken reflections drifted through his mind, as he yawned and prepared to sleep. His brain brought up events of the day—a missed shot, a good shot, lunch under a haystack with Mary and Fayre-Michell's niece. She was smart and showy and slangy—cheap every way compared with Mary. What would his wife think if she knew he was so near? Come to him for certain. He cordially hoped that he might not be recalled to his ship; but there was a possibility of it. It would be rather a lark to show the governor over the Indomitable. She was a "hush-hush" ship—one of the wonders of the Navy still. Funny that the Italian roof of the Grey Room looked like a dome, though it was really flat. A cunning trick of perspective.

It was a still and silent night, moonless, very dark, and very tranquil. He went to the window to throw it open.

Only a solitary being waked long that night at Chadlands, and only a solitary mind suffered tribulation. But into the small hours Henry Lennox endured the companionship of disquiet thoughts. He could not sleep, and his brain, clear enough, retraced no passage from the past day. Indeed the events of the day had sunk into remote time. He was only concerned with the present, and he wondered while he worried that he should be worrying. Yet a proleptic instinct made him look forward. He had neither lied nor exaggerated to May. From the moment of losing the toss, he honestly experienced a strong, subjective impression of danger arising out of the proposed attack on the mysteries of the Grey Room. It was, indeed, that consciousness of greater possibilities in the adventure than May admitted or imagined which made Lennox so insistent. Looking back, he perceived many things, and chiefly that he had taken a wrong line, and approached Mary's husband from a fatal angle. Too late he recognized his error. It was inevitable that a hint of suspected danger would confirm the sailor in his resolution; and that such a hint should follow the spin of the coin against Lennox, and be accompanied by the assurance that, had he won, Henry would have proceeded, despite his intuitions, to do what he now begged Tom not to do—that was a piece of clumsy work which he deeply regretted.

At the hour when his own physical forces were lowest, his errors of diplomacy forced themselves upon his mind. He wasted much time, as all men do upon their beds, in antici-pating to-morrow; in considering what is going to happen, or what is not; in weighing their own future words and deeds given a variety of contingencies. For reason, which at first kept him, despite his disquiet, in the region of the rational, grew weaker with Henry as the night advanced; the shadow of trouble deep-ened as his weary wits lost their balance to combat it. The premonition was as formless and amorphous as a cloud, and, though he could not see any shape to his fear, or define its limi-tations, it grew darker ere he slept. He considered what might happen and, putting aside any lesser disaster, tried to imagine what the morning would bring if May actually succumbed.

For the moment the size of such an imaginary disaster served curiously to lessen his uneasiness. Pushed to extremities, the idea became merely absurd. He won a sort of comfort from such an outrageous proposition, because it brought him back to the solid ground of reason and the assurance that some things simply do not happen. From this extravagant summit of horror, his fears gradually receded. Such a waking nightmare even quieted his nerves when it was past; for if a possibility pres-ents a ludicrous side, then its horror must diminish by so much.

Moreover, Henry told himself that if the threat of a disaster so absolute could really be felt by him, it was his duty to rise at once, intervene, and, if necessary, summon his uncle and force May to leave the Grey Room immediately.

This idea amused him again and offered another jest. The tragedy really resolved into jests. He found himself smiling at the picture of May being treated like a disobedient schoolboy. But if that happened, and Tom was proclaimed the sinner, what must be Henry's own fate? To win the reputation of an unsportsmanlike sneak in Mary's opinion as well as Tom's. He certainly could call upon nobody to help him now. But he might go and look up May himself. That would be very sharply resented, however. He travelled round and round in circles, then asked himself what he would do and say to-morrow if anything happened to Tom—nothing, of course, fatal, but something perhaps so grave that May himself would be unable to explain it. In that case Henry could only state facts exactly as they had occurred. But there would be a deuce of a muddle if he had to make statements and describe the exact sequence of recent incidents. Already he forgot the exact sequence. It seemed ages since he parted from May. He broke off there, rose, drank a glass of water, and lighted a cigarette. He shook himself into wakefulness, condemned himself for this debauch of weak-minded thinking, found the time to be three o'clock, and brushed the whole cobweb tangle from his mind. He knew that sudden warmth after cold will often induce sleep—a fact proved by incidents of his campaigns—so he trudged up and down and opened his window and let the cool breath of the night chill his forehead and breast for five minutes.

This action calmed him, and he headed himself off from returning to the subject. He felt that mental dread and discomfort were only waiting to break out again; but he smothered them, returned to bed, and succeeded in keeping his mind on neutral-tinted matter until he fell asleep.

He woke again before he was called, rose and went to his bath. He took it cold, and it refreshed him and cleared his head, for he had a headache. Everything was changed, and the phantoms of his imagination remained only as memories to be laughed at. He no longer felt alarm or anxiety. He dressed presently, and guessing that Tom, always the first to rise, might already be out of doors, he strolled on to the terrace presently to meet him there.

Already he speculated whether an apology was due from him to May, or whether he might himself expect one. It didn't matter. He knew perfectly well that Tom was all right now, and that was the only thing that signified.

CHAPTER III.

AT THE ORIEL

Chadlands sprang into existence when the manor houses of England—save for the persistence of occasional embattled parapets and other warlike survivals of unrestful days now past— had obeyed the laws of architectural evolution, and begun to approach a future of cleanliness and comfort, rising to luxury hitherto unknown. The development of this ancient mass was displayed in plan as much as in elevation, and, at its date, the great mansion had stood for the last word of perfection, when men thought on large lines and the conditions of labour made possible achievements now seldom within the power of a private purse. Much had since been done, but the main architectural features were preserved, though the interior of the great house was transformed.

The manor of Chadlands extended to some fifty thousand acres lying in a river valley between the heights of Haldon on the east and the frontiers of Dartmoor westerly. The little township was connected by a branch with the Great Western

Railway, and the station lay five miles from the manor house. No more perfect parklands, albeit on a modest scale, existed in South Devon, and the views of the surrounding heights and great vale opening from the estate caused pleasure alike to those contented with obvious beauty and the small number of spectators who understood the significance of what constitutes really distinguished landscape.

Eastward, long slopes of herbage and drifts of azaleas—a glorious harmony of gold, scarlet, and orange in June—sloped upwards to larch woods; while the gardens of pleasure, watered by a little trout stream, spread beneath the manor house, and behind it rose hot-houses and the glass and walled gardens of fruit and vegetables. To the south and west opened park and vale, where receded forest and fallow lands, until the grey ramparts of the moor ascending beyond them hemmed in the picture.

Sir Walter Lennox had devoted himself to the sporting side of the estate and had made it famous in this respect. His father, less interested in shooting and hunting, had devoted time and means to the flower gardens, and rendered them as rich as was possible in his day; while earlier yet, Sir Walter's grandfather had been more concerned for the interior, and had done much to enrich and beautify it.

A great terrace stretched between the south front and a balustrade of granite, that separated it from the gardens spreading at a lower level. Here walked Henry Lennox and sought Tom May. It was now past eight o'clock on Sunday morning, and he found himself alone. The sun, breaking through heaviness of morning clouds, had risen clear of Haldon Hills and cast a radiance, still dimmed by vapour, over the glow of the autumn trees. Subdued sounds of birds came from the glades below, and far distant, from the scrub at the edge of the woods, pheasants were crowing.

The morning sparkled, and, in a scene so fair, Henry found his spirits rise. Already the interview with Mary's husband on the preceding night seemed remote and unreal. He was, however, conscious that he had made an ass of himself, but he did not much mind, for it could not be said that May had shone, either.

He called him, and, for reply, an old spaniel emerged from beneath, climbed a flight of broad steps that ascended to the terrace, and paddled up to Henry, wagging his tail. He was a very ancient hero, whose record among the wild duck still remained a worthy memory and won him honour in his declining days. The age of "Prince" remained doubtful, but he was decrepit now— gone in the hams and suffering from cataract of both eyes—a disease to which it is impossible to minister in a dog. But his life was good to him; he still got about, slept in the sun, and shared the best his master's dish could offer. Sir Walter adored him, and immediately felt uneasy if the creature did not appear when summoned. Often, had he been invisible too long, his master would wander whistling round his haunts. Then he would find him, or be himself found, and feel easy again.

"Prince" went in to the open window of the breakfast-room, while Henry, moved by a thought, walked round the eastern angle of the house and looked up at the oriel window of the Grey Room, where it hung aloft on the side of the wall, like a brilliant bubble, and flashed with the sunshine that now irradiated the casement. To his surprise he saw the window was thrown open and that May, still in his pyjamas, knelt on the cushioned recess within and looked out at the morning.

"Good lord, old chap!" he cried, "Needn't ask you if you have slept. It's nearly nine o'clock."

But the other made no response whatever. He continued to gaze far away over Henry's head at the sunrise, while the morning breeze moved his dark hair.

"Tom! Wake up!" shouted Lennox again; but still the other did not move a muscle. Then Henry noticed that he was unusually pale, and something about his unwinking eyes also seemed foreign to an intelligent expression. They were set, and no movement of light played upon them. It seemed that the watcher was in a trance. Henry felt his heart jump, and a sensation of alarm sharpened his thought. For him the morning was suddenly transformed, and fearing an evil thing had indeed befallen the other, he turned to the terrace and entered the breakfast-room from it. The time was now five minutes to nine, and as unfailing punctuality had ever been a foible of Sir Walter, his guests usually respected it. Most of them were already assembled, and Mary May, who was just stepping into the garden, asked Henry if he had seen her husband.

"He's always the first to get up and the last to go to bed," she said.

Bidding her good-morning, but not answering her question, the young man hastened through the room and ascended to the corridor. Beneath, Ernest Travers, a being of fussy temperament with a heart of gold, spoke to Colonel Vane. Travers was clad in Sunday black, for he respected tradition.

"Forgive me, won't you, but this is your first visit, and you don't look much like church."

"Must we go to church, too?" asked the colonel blankly. He was still a year under forty, but had achieved distinction in the war. "There is no 'must' about it, but Sir Walter would appreciate the effort on your part. He likes his guests to go. He is one of those men who are a light to this generation—an ancient light, if you like, but a shining one. He loves sound maxims. You may say he runs his life on sound maxims. He lives charitably with all men and it puzzles him, as it puzzles me, to understand the growing doubt, the class prejudice—nay, class hatred the failure of trust and the increasing tension and uneasiness between employer and employed. He and I are agreed that the tribulations of the present time can be traced to two disasters only—the lack of goodwill—as shown in the proletariat, whose leaders teach them to respect nobody, and the weakening hold of religion as also revealed in the proletariat. Now, to combat these things and set a good example is our duty—nay, our privilege. Don't you think so?"

Such a lecture on an empty stomach depressed the colonel. He looked uneasy and anxious.

"I'll come, of course, if he'd like it; but I'm afraid I shared my men's dread of church parade, though our padre was a merciful being on the whole and fairly sensible."

Overhead, Henry had tried the door of the Grey Room, and found it locked. As he did so, the gong sounded for breakfast. Masters always performed upon it. First he woke a preliminary whisper of the great bronze disc, then deepened the note to a genial and mellow roar, and finally calmed it down again until it faded gently into silence. He spoke of the gong as a musical instrument, and declared the art of sounding it was a gift that few men could acquire.

Neither movement nor response rewarded the summons of Lennox, and now in genuine alarm, he went below again, stopped Fred Caunter, the footman, and asked him to call out Sir Walter.

Fred waited until his master had said a brief grace before meat; then he stepped to his side and explained, that his nephew desired to see him.

"Good patience! What's the matter?" asked the old man as he rose and joined Henry in the hall.

Then his nephew spoke, and indicated his alarm. He stammered a little, but strove to keep calm and state facts clearly.

"It's like this. I'm afraid you'll be rather savage, but I can't talk now. Tom and I had a yarn when you'd gone to bed, and he was awfully keen to spend the night in the Grey Room."

"I did not wish it."

"I know—we were wrong—but we were both death on it, and we tossed up, and he won."

"Where is he?"

"Up there now, looking out of the window. I've called him and made a row at the door, but he doesn't answer. He's locked himself in, apparently."

"What have you done, Henry? We must get to him instantly. Tell Caunter—no, I will. Don't breathe a syllable of this to anybody unless necessity arises. Don't tell Mary."

Sir Walter beckoned the footman, bade him get some tools and ascend quickly to the Grey Room. He then went up beside his nephew, while Fred, bristling with excitement, hastened to the toolroom. He was a handy man, had been at sea during the war, and now returned to his old employment. His slow brain moved backwards, and he remembered that this was a task he had already performed ten or more years before. Then the ill-omened chamber had revealed a dead woman. Who was in it now? Caunter guessed readily enough.

Lennox spoke to his uncle as they approached the locked door.

"It was only a lark, just to clear the room of its bad character and have a laugh at your expense this morning. But I'm afraid he's ill—fainted or something. He turned in about one o'clock. I was rather bothered, and couldn't explain to myself why, but—"

"Don't chatter!" answered the other. "You have both done a very wrong thing and should have respected my wishes."

At the door he called loudly.

"Let us in at once, Tom, please! I am much annoyed! If

this is a jest, it has gone far enough—and too far! I blame you severely!"

But none replied. Absolute silence held the Grey Room.

Then came the footman with a frail of tools. The task could not be performed in a moment, and Sir Walter, desirous above all things to create no uneasiness at the breakfast-table, determined to go down again. But he was too late, for his daughter had already suspected something. She was not anxious but puzzled that her husband tarried. She came up the stairs with a letter.

"I'm going to find Tom," she said. "It's not like him to be so lazy. Here's a letter from the ship, and I'm awfully afraid he may have to go back."

"Mary," said her father, "come here a moment."

He drew her under a great window which threw light into the corridor.

"You must summon your nerve and pluck, my girl! I'm very much afraid that something has gone amiss with Tom. I know nothing yet, but last night, it seems, after we had gone to bed, he and Henry determined that one of them should sleep in the Grey Room."

"Father! Was he there, and I so near him—sleeping in the very next room?"

"He was there—and is there. He is not well. Henry saw him looking out of the window five minutes ago, but he was, I fear, unconscious."

"Let me go to him," she said.

"I will do so first. It will be wiser. Run down and ask Ernest to join me. Do not be alarmed; I dare say it is nothing at all."

Her habit of obedience prompted her to do as he desired instantly, but she descended like lightning, called Travers, and returned with him.

"I will ask you to come in with me, Ernest," explained Sir Walter. "My son-in-law slept in the Grey Room last night, and he does not respond to our calls this morning. The door is locked and we are breaking it open."

"But you expressly refused him permission to do so, Walter."

"I did—you heard me. Let sleeping dogs lie is a very good motto, but young men will be young men. I hope, however, nothing serious—"

He stopped, for Caunter had forced the door and burst it inward with a crash. During the moment's silence that followed they heard the key spring into the room and strike the wainscot. The place was flooded with sunshine, and seemed to welcome them with genial light and attractive art. The furniture revealed its rich grain and beautiful modelling; the cherubs carved on the great chairs seemed to dance where the light flashed on their little, rounded limbs. The silvery walls were bright, and the huge roses that tumbled over them appeared to revive and display their original color at the touch of the sun.

On a chair beside the bed stood an extinguished candle, Tom's watch, and Henry's revolver. The sailor's dressing-gown was still folded where he had placed it; his rug was at the foot of the bed. He himself knelt in the recess at the open window upon the settee that ran beneath. His position was natural; one arm held the window-ledge and steadied him, and his back was turned to Sir Walter and Travers, who first entered the room.

Henry held Mary back and implored her to wait a moment, but she shook off his hand and followed her father.

Sir Walter it was who approached Tom and grasped his arm. In so doing he disturbed the balance of the body, which fell back and was caught by the two men. Its weight bore Ernest Travers to the ground, but Henry was in time to save both the quick and the dead. For Tom May had expired many hours before. His face was of an ivory whiteness, his mouth closed. No sign of fear, but rather a profound astonishment sat upon his features. His eyes were opened and dim. In them, too, was frozen a sort of speechless amazement. How long he had been dead they knew not, but none were in doubt of the fact. His wife, too, perceived it. She went to where he now lay, put her arms around his neck, and fainted.

Others were moving outside, and the murmur of voices reached the Grey Room. It was one of those tragic situations when everybody desires to be of service, and when well-meaning and small-minded people are often hurt unintentionally and never forget it, putting fancied affronts before the incidents that caused them.

The man lay dead and his wife unconscious upon his body.

Sir Walter rose to the occasion as best he might, issued orders, and begged all who heard him to obey without question. He and his friend Travers lifted Mary and carried her to her room. It was her nursery of old. Here they put her on her bed, and sent Caunter for Mrs. Travers and Mary's old servant, Jane Bond. She had recovered consciousness before the women reached her. Then they returned to the dead, and the master of Chadlands urged those standing on the stairs and in the corridor to go back to their breakfast and their duties.

"You can do no good," he said. "I will only ask Vane to help us."

Fayre-Michell spoke, while the colonel came forward.

"Forgive me, Sir Walter, but if it is anything psychical, I ask, as a member—"

"For Heaven's sake do as I wish," returned the other. "My son-in-law is dead. What more there is to know, you'll hear later. I want Vane, because he is a powerful man and can help Henry and my butler. We have to carry—"

He broke off.

"Dead!" gasped the visitor.

Then he hastened downstairs. Presently they lifted the sailor among them, and got him to his own room. They could not dispose him in a comely position—a fact that specially troubled Sir Walter—and Masters doubted not that the doctor would be able to do it.

Henry Lennox started as swiftly as possible for the house of the physician, four miles off. He took a small motor-car, did the journey along empty roads in twelve minutes, and was back again with Dr. Mannering in less than half an hour.

The people, whose visit of pleasure was thus painfully brought to a close, moved about whispering on the terrace. They had as yet heard no details, and were considering whether it would be possible to get off at once, or necessary to wait until the morrow.

Their natural desire was to depart, since they could not be of any service to the stricken household; but no facilities existed on Sunday. They walked about in little groups. One or two, desiring to smoke but feeling that to do so would appear callous, descended into the seclusion of the garden. Then Ernest Travers joined them. He was important, but could only tell them that May had disobeyed his father-in-law, slept in the Grey Room, and died there. He gave them details and declared that in his opinion it would be unseemly to attempt to leave until the following day.

"Sir Walter would feel it," he said. "He is bearing up well. He will lunch with us. My wife tells me that Mary, Mrs. May, is very sadly. That is natural—an awful blow. I find myself incapable of grasping it. To think of so much boyish good spirits and such vitality extinguished in this way."

"Can we do anything on earth for them?" asked Millicent Fayre-Michell.

"Nothing—nothing. If I may advise, I think we had all better go to church. By so doing we get out of the way for a time and please dear Sir Walter. I shall certainly go."

They greeted the suggestion—indeed, clutched at it. Their bewildered minds welcomed action. They were hushed and perturbed. Death, crashing in upon them thus, left them more than uncomfortable. Some, at the bottom of their souls, felt almost indignant that an event so horrible should have disturbed the level tenor of their lives. They shared the most profound sympathy for the sufferers as well as for themselves. Some discovered that their own physical bodies were upset, too, and felt surprised at the depth of their emotions.

"It isn't as if it were natural," Felix Fayre-Michell persisted. "Don't imagine that for a moment."

"It's too creepy—I can't believe it," declared his niece. She was incapable of suffering much for anybody, and her excitement had a flavour not wholly bitter. She saw herself describing these events at other house parties. It would be unfair to say that she was enjoying herself; still she knew nobody at Chadlands very well, it was her first visit, and adventures are, after all, adventures. Her uncle discussed the psychic significance of the tragedy, and gave instances of similar events. One or two listened to him for lack of anything better to do. There was a general sensation of blankness. They were all thrown. Life had let them down. Under the circumstances, to most of them it seemed an excellent idea to go to church. Vane joined them presently. He was able to give them many details and excite their interest. They crowded round him, and he spoke nakedly. Death was nothing to him—he had seen so much. They heard the motor return with Dr. Mannering.

"We're so out of it," said Mr. Miles Handford, a stout man from Yorkshire—a wealthy landowner and sportsman.

He was unaccustomed to be out of anything in his environment, and he showed actual irritation.

"Thank Heaven we are, I should think!" answered another; and the first speaker frowned at him.

Ernest Travers joined them presently. He had put on a black tie and wore black gloves and a silk hat.

"If you accompany me," he said, "I can show you the short way by a field path. It cuts off half a mile. I have told Sir Walter we all go to church, and he asked me if we would like the motors; but I felt, the day being fine, you would agree with me that we might walk. He is terribly crushed, but taking it like the man he is."

Miles Handford and Fayre-Michell followed the church party in the rear, and relieved their minds by criticizing Mr. Travers.

"Officious ass!" said the stout man. "A typical touch that black tie! A decent-minded person would have felt this appalling tragedy far too much to think of such a trifle. I hope I shall never see the brute again."

"It seems too grotesque marching to church like a lot of children, because he tells us to do so," murmured Fayre-Michell.

"I don't want to go. I only want distraction. In fact, I don't think I shall go," added Mr. Handford. But a woman urged him to do so.

"Sir Walter would like it," she said.

"It's all very sad and very exasperating indeed," declared the Yorkshireman; "and it shows, if that wanted showing, that there's far, far less consideration among young men for their elders than there used to be in my young days. If my father-in-law had told me not to do a thing, the very wish to do it would have disappeared at once."

"Sir Walter was as clear as need be," added Felix. "We all heard him. Then the young fool—Heaven forgive him—behind everybody's back goes and plays with fire in this insane way."

"The selfishness! Just look at the inconvenience—the upset—
the suffering to his relations and the worry for all of us. All our
plans must be altered—everything upset, life for the moment
turned upside down—a woman's heart broken very likely—
and all for a piece of disobedient folly. Such things make one
out of tune with Providence. They oughtn't to happen. They
don't happen in Yorkshire. Devonshire appears to be a slacker's
county. It's the air, I shouldn't wonder."

"Education, and law and order, and the discipline inculcated in
the Navy ought to have prevented this," continued Fayre-Michell.
"Who ever heard of a sailor disobeying—except Nelson?"

"He's paid, poor fellow," said his niece, who walked beside him.

"We have all paid," declared the north countryman. "We
have all paid the price; and the price has been a great deal of
suffering and discomfort and stress of mind that we ought not
have been called upon to endure. One resents such things in a
stable world."

"Well, I'm not going to church, anyway. I must smoke for my
nerves. I'm a psychic myself, and I react to a thing of this sort,"
replied Fayre-Michell.

From a distant stile between two fields Mr. Travers, some
hundred yards ahead, was waving directions and pointing to
the left.

"Go to Jericho!" snapped Mr. Handford, but not loud enough
for Ernest Travers to hear him.

A little ring of bells throbbed thin music. It rose and fell on
the easterly breeze and a squat grey tower, over which floated a
white ensign on a flagstaff, appeared upon a little knoll of trees
in the midst of the village of Chadlands.

Presently the bells stopped, and the flag was brought down to
half-mast. Mr. Travers had reached the church.

"A maddening sort of man," said Miles Handford, who

marked these phenomena. "Be sure Sir Walter never told him to do anything of that sort. He has taken it upon himself—a theatrical mind. If I were the vicar—"

Elsewhere Dr. Mannering heard what Henry Lennox could tell him as they returned to the manor house together. He displayed very deep concern combined with professional interest. He recalled the story that Sir Walter had related on the previous night.

"Not a shadow of evidence—a perfectly healthy little woman; and it will be the same here as sure as I'm alive," he said. "To think—we shot side by side yesterday, and I remarked his fine physique and wonderful high spirits—a big, tough fellow. How's poor Mary?"

"She is pretty bad, but keeping her nerve, as she would be sure to do," declared the other.

Sir Walter was with his daughter when Mannering arrived. The doctor had been a crony of the elder for many years. He was about the average of a country physician—a hard-bitten, practical man who loved his profession, loved sport, and professed conservative principles. Experience stood in place of high qualifications, but he kept in touch with medical progress, to the extent of reading about it and availing himself of improved methods and preparations when opportunity offered. He examined the dead man very carefully, indicated how his posture might be rendered more normal, and satisfied himself that human power was incapable of restoring the vanished life. He could discover no visible indication of violence and no apparent excuse for Tom May's sudden end. He listened with attention to the little that Henry Lennox could tell him, and then went to see Mary May and her father.

The young wife had grown more collected, but she was dazed rather than reconciled to her fate; her mind had not yet absorbed the full extent of her sorrow. She talked incessantly and dwelt on trivialities, as people will under a weight of events too large to measure or discuss.

"I am going to write to Tom's father," she said. "This will be an awful blow to him. He was wrapped up in Tom. And to think that I was troubling about his letter! He will never see the sea he loved so much again. He always hated that verse in the Bible that says there will be no more sea. I was asleep so near him last night. Yet I never heard him cry out or anything."

Mannering talked gently to her.

"Be sure he did not cry out. He felt no pain, no shock—I am sure of that. To die is no hardship to the dead, remember. He is at peace, Mary. You must come and see him presently. Your father will call you soon. There is just a look of wonder in his face—no fear, no suffering. Keep that in mind."

"He could not have felt fear. He knew of nothing that a brave man might fear, except doing wrong. Nobody knows how good he was but me. His father loved him fiercely, passionately; but he never knew how good he was, because Tom did not think quite like old Mr. May. I must write and say that Tom is dangerously ill, and cannot recover. That will break it to him. Tom was the only earthly affection he had. It will be terrible when he comes."

They left her, and, after they had gone, she rose, fell on her knees, and so remained, motionless and tearless, for a long time. Through her own desolation, as yet unrealized, there still persisted the thought of her husband's father. It seemed that her mind could dwell on his isolation, while powerless to present the truth of her husband's death to her. By some strange mental operation, not unbeneficent, she saw his grief more vividly than as yet she felt her own. She rose presently, quick-eared to wait the call, and went to her desk in the window. Then she wrote a letter to her father-in-law, and pictured his ministering at that moment to his church. Her inclination was to soften the blow, yet she knew that could only be a cruel kindness. She told him, therefore, that his son must die. Then she remembered that he was so near. A telegram must go rather than a letter, and he would be at Chadlands before nightfall. She destroyed her letter and set about a telegram. Jane Bond came in, and she asked her to dispatch the telegram as quickly as possible. Her old nurse, an elderly spinster, to whom Mary was the first consideration in existence, had brought her a cup of soup and some toast. It had seemed to Jane the right thing to do.

Mary thanked her and drank a little. She passed through a mental phase as of dreaming—a sensation familiar in sleep; but she knew that this was not a sleeping but a waking experience. She waited for her father, yet dreaded to hear him return. She thought of human footsteps and the difference between them. She remembered that she would never hear Tom's long stride again.

It often broke into a run, she remembered, as he approached her; and she would often run toward him, too—to banish the space that separated them. She blamed herself bitterly that she had decreed to sleep in her old nursery. She had loved it so, and the small bed that had held her from childhood; yet, if she had slept with him, this might not have happened.

"To think that only a wall separated us!" she kept saying to herself. "And I sleeping and dreaming of him, and he dying only a few yards away."

Death was no disaster for Tom, so the doctor had said. What worthless wisdom! And perhaps not even wisdom. Who knows what a disaster death may be? And who would ever know what he had felt at the end, or what his mind had suffered if time had been given him to understand that he was going to die?

She worked herself into agony, lost self-control at last and wept, with Jane Bond's arms round her.

"And I was so troubled, because I thought he had been called back to his ship!" she said.

"He's called to a better place than a ship, dear love," sobbed Jane.

After they left her, Sir Walter and Dr. Mannering had entered the Grey Room for a moment and, standing there, spoke together.

"I have a strange consciousness that I am living over the past again," declared the physician. "Things were just so when that poor woman, Nurse Forrester—you remember."

"Yes. I felt the same when Caunter was breaking open the door. I faced the worst from the beginning, for the moment I heard what he had done, I somehow knew that my unfortunate son-in-law was dead. I directly negatived his suggestion last night, and never dreamed that he would have gone on with it when he knew my wish."

"Doubtless he did not realize how much in earnest you were on the subject. This may well prove as impossible to understand as the nurse's death. I do not say it will; but I suspect it will. A perfectly healthy creature cut off in a moment and nothing to show us why—absolutely nothing."

"A death without a cause—a negation of science surely?"

"There is a cause, but I do not think this dreadful tragedy will reveal it," answered the doctor. "I pray it may, however, for all our sakes," he continued. "It is impossible to say how deeply I feel this for her, but also for you, and myself, too. He was one of the best, a good sportsman and a good man."

"And a great loss to the Service," added Sir Walter. "I have not considered all this means yet. My thoughts are centred on Mary."

"You must let me spare you all I can, my friend. There will be an inquest, of course, and an inquiry. Also a post-mortem. Shall I communicate with Dr. Mordred to-day, or would you prefer that somebody else—"

"Somebody else. The most famous man you know. From no disrespect to Dr. Mordred, or to you, Mannering. You understand that. But I should like an independent examination by some great authority, some one who knew nothing of the former case. This is an appalling thing to happen. I don't know where to begin thinking."

"Do not put too great a strain upon yourself. Leave it to those who will come to the matter with all their wits and without your personal sorrow. An independent inquirer is certainly best, one who, as you say, knows nothing about the former case."

"I don't know where to begin thinking," repeated the other. "Such a thing upsets one's preconceived opinions. I had always regarded my aversion to this room as a human weakness—a thing to be conquered. Look round you. Would it be possible to imagine an apartment with less of evil suggestion?"

The other made a perfunctory examination, went into every corner, tapped the walls and stared at the ceiling. The clean morning light showed its intricate pattern of interwoven circles converging from the walls to the centre, and so creating a sense of a lofty dome instead of a flat surface. In the centre was a boss of a conventional lily flower opening its petals.

"The room should not be touched till after the inquest, I think. Indeed, if I may advise, you will do well to leave it just as it is for the police to see."

"They will want to see it, I imagine?"

"Unless you communicate direct with Scotland Yard, ask for a special inquiry, and beg that the local men are not employed. There is reason in that, for it is quite certain that nobody here would be of any greater use to you than they were before."

"Act for me then, please. Explain that money is no object, and ask them to send the most accomplished and experienced men in the service. But they are only concerned with crime. This may be outside their scope."

"We cannot say as to that. We cannot even assert that this is not a crime. We know nothing."

"A crime needs a criminal, Mannering."

"That is so; but what would be criminal, if human agency were responsible for it, might, nevertheless, be the work of forces to which the word criminal cannot be applied."

Sir Walter stared at him.

"Is it possible you suggest a supernatural cause for this?"

The doctor shook his head.

"Emphatically not, though I am not a materialist, as you are aware. My generation of practitioners has little difficulty in reconciling our creed with our cult, though few of the younger men are able to do so, I admit. But science is science, and not for a moment do I imagine anything supernatural here. I think, however, there are unconscious forces at work, and those responsible for setting those forces in action would be criminals without a doubt, if they knew what they were doing. The man who fires a rifle at an animal, if he hits and kills it, is the destroyer, though he may operate from half a mile away. On the other hand, the agents may be unconscious of what they are doing."

"There is no human being in this house for whom I would not answer."

"I know it. We beat the wind. It will be time enough to consider presently. Indeed, I should rather that you strove to relieve your mind of the problem. You have enough to do without that. Leave it to those professionally trained in such mysteries. If a man is responsible for this atrocious thing, then it should be within the reach of man's wits to find him. We failed before; but this time no casual examination of this place, or the antecedents of your son-in-law's life, will serve the purpose. We must go to the bottom, or, rather, skilled minds, trained to do so, must go to the bottom. They will approach the subject from a different angle. They will come unprejudiced and unperturbed. If there has been foul play, they will find it out. In my opinion it is incredible that they will be baffled."

"The best men engaged in such work must come to help us. I cannot bring myself to believe the room is haunted, and that this is the operation of an evil force outside Nature, yet permitted by the Creator to destroy human life. The idea is too horrible—it revolts me, Mannering."

"Well, it may do so. Banish any such irrational thought from your mind. It is not worthy of you. I must go now. I will telegraph to London—to Sir Howard Fellowes—also, I think to the State authorities on forensic medicine. A Government analyst must do his part. Shall I communicate with Scotland Yard to-day?"

"Leave that until the evening. You will come again to see Mary, please."

"Most certainly I shall. At three o'clock I should have a reply to my messages. I will go into Newton Abbot and telephone from there."

"I thank you, Mannering. I wish it were possible to do more myself. My mind is cruelly shaken. This awful experience has made an old man of me."

"Don't say that. It is awful enough, I admit. But life is full of awful things. Would that you might have escaped them!"

"Henry will help you, if it is in his power. It would be well if we could give him something to do. He feels guilty in a way. I have little time to observe other people; but—"

"He's all right. He can run into Newton with me now. It looks to me as though his own life had hung on the pitch of a coin. They tossed up! After that—so he tells me—he tried to dissuade your son-in-law, but failed. Lennox is rather cowed and dismayed—naturally. The young, however, survive mental and physical disasters and recover in the most amazing manner. Their mental recuperation is on a par with their bodily powers of recovery. Nature is on their side. Let me urge you to go down and take food. If you can even lunch with your party I should. It will distract your mind."

Sir Walter declared that he had intended to do so.

"I am an old soldier," he said. "It shall not be thought I evade my obligations for personal sorrow. As for this room, it is accursed and I am in a mind to destroy it utterly."

"Wait—wait. We shall see what our fellow-men can find out for us. Do not think, because I am practical and business-like, I am not feeling this. Seldom have I had such a shock in nearly forty years' work. You know, without my telling you, how deep and heartfelt is my sympathy. I feel for you both from my soul."

"I am sure of that. I will try and forget myself for the present. I must go to my guests. I am very sorry for them also. It is a fearful experience to crash upon their party of pleasure."

"I hope Travers may stay. He is a comfort to you, is he not?"

"Nobody can be a comfort just now. I shall not ask him to stay. Fortunately Henry is here. He will stop for the present. Mary is all that matters. I shall take her away as quickly as possible and devote my every thought to her."

"I'm sure you will. It is a sad duty, but may prove a very necessary one. Their devotion was absolute. It must go hard with her when she realizes the whole meaning of this."

He went his way, and Sir Walter returned to his child again. With her he visited the dead, when told that he could do so. She was now very self-controlled. She stopped a little while only beside her husband.

"How beautiful and happy he looks," she said. "But what I loved is gone; and, going, it has changed all the rest. This is not Tom—only the least part of him."

Her father bowed his head.

"I felt so when your mother died, my dearest child."

Then she knelt down and put her hand on the hand of the dead man and prayed. Her father knelt beside her, and it was he, not the young widow, who wept.

She rose presently.

"I can think of him better away from him now," she said. "I will not see him again."

They returned to her old nursery, and he told her that he was going to face life and take the head of his table at luncheon.

"How brave of you, dear father," she said. Sir Walter waited for the gong to sound, but it did not, and he rebuked himself for thinking that it would sound. Masters had a more correct sense of the fitness of things than he. He thought curiously upon this incident, and suspected that he must be unhinged a little. Then he remembered a thing that he had desired to say to Mary and returned to her.

"I do not wish you to sleep in this room to-night, my darling," he said.

"Jane has begged me not to. I am going to sleep with her," she answered.

CHAPTER IV.

"BY THE HAND OF GOD"

Sir Walter always remembered that Sunday luncheon and declared that it reminded him of a very painful experience in his early life. When big-game shooting in South Africa, he had once been tossed by a wounded buffalo bull. By good chance the creature threw him into a gully some feet lower than the surrounding bush. Thus it lost him, and he was safe from destruction. There, however, he remained with a broken leg for some hours until rescued; and during that time the mosquitoes caused him unspeakable torments.

To-day the terrible disaster of the morning became temporarily overshadowed by the necessity of enduring his friends' comments upon it. The worst phase of the ordeal was their pity. Sir Walter had never been pitied in his life, and detested the experience. This stream of sympathy and the chastened voices much oppressed him. He was angry with himself also, for a guilty conviction that, in truth, the interest of the visitors exceeded their grief. He felt it base to suspect them of any such thing; but the buzz of their polite expressions, combined with their cautious questions and evident thirst for knowledge, caused him exquisite uneasiness.

They all wanted to know everything he could tell them concerning Tom May. Had he enemies? Was it conceivable that he might have even bitter and unscrupulous enemies?

"Dear Mary is keeping up splendidly," said Mrs. Travers. "She is magnificent. Thank Heaven I have been some little help to her."

"You have, Nelly, without a doubt."

"Do try to eat more, Walter," urged Ernest Travers. "Much lies before you. Indeed, the worst has yet to come. You must keep up for all our sakes. How thankfully I would share your load if I could!"

"I hope you are going to make this an official matter, Sir Walter, and communicate with the Society for Psychical Research," urged Felix Fayre-Michell. "It is just a case for them. In fact, when this gets known widely, as it must, of course, a great many skilled inquirers will wish to visit Chadlands and spend a night in the room."

"The police will have to be considered first," declared Colonel Vane. "This is, of course, a police affair. I should think they will so regard it. There is the Service, too. The Admiralty will be sure to do something."

"Is he to be buried at Chadlands? I suppose so, poor fellow," murmured Ernest Travers. "I think your family graves so distinguished, Walter—so simple and fine and modest—just perfectly kept, grassy mounds, and simple inscriptions. I was looking at them after service to-day. The vicar made a very tactful allusion to the great grief that had overtaken the lord of the manor at the end of his sermon."

Henry assisted his uncle to the best of his power. It was he who went into the question of the Sunday service from the neighboring market town, and proved, to the relief of Colonel Vane and Mr. Miles Handford, that they might leave in comfort before nightfall and catch a train to London.

"A car is going in later, to meet poor Tom's father," he said, "and if it's any convenience, it would take you both."

The pair thankfully agreed.

Then Colonel Vane interested Sir Walter in spite of himself. The latter had spoken of an inquiry, and Vane urged a distinguished name upon him.

"Do get Peter Hardcastle if you can," he said. "He's absolutely top hole at this sort of thing at present—an amazing beggar."

"I seem to have heard the name."

"Who hasn't? It was he who got to the bottom of that weird murder in Yorkshire."

"It was weird," said Handford. "I knew intimate friends of the murdered man."

"A crime for which no logical reason existed," continued the colonel. "It puzzled everybody, till Hardcastle succeeded where his superior officers at Scotland Yard had failed. I believe he's still young. But that was less amazing than the German spy— you remember now, Sir Walter? The spy had been too clever for England and France—thanks to a woman who helped him. Peter Hardcastle got to know her; then he actually disguised himself as the woman—of course without her knowledge— arrested her, and kept an appointment that she had made with the spy. What was the spy called? I forget."

"Wundt," said Felix Fayre-Michell.

"No, I don't think so. Hardt or Hardfelt, or something like that."

"Anyway, a jolly wonderful thing. He's the first man at this business, and I hope you'll be able to secure him."

"If he comes, Sir Walter, don't let it be known that he is here. Keep it a secret. If Hardcastle could come down as your guest, and nobody know he was here, it might help him to succeed."

"And if he fails, then I hope you'll invite the Psychical Research Society."

Sir Walter let the chatter flow past him; but he concentrated on the name of Peter Hardcastle. He remembered the story of the spy, and the sensation it had aroused.

Millicent Fayre-Michell also remembered it.

"Mr. Hardcastle declined to let his photograph be published in the halfpenny papers, I remember," she said. "That struck me as so wonderful. There was a reason given—that he did not wish the public to know him by sight. I believe he is never seen as himself, and that he makes up just as easily to look like a woman as a man."

"Some people believe he is a woman."

"No! You don't say that?"

"To have made up as that German's friend and so actually reached his presence—nay, secured him! It is certainly one of the most remarkable pages in the annals of crime," said Ernest Travers.

"Is he attached to Scotland Yard still, or does he work independently?" asked Miles Handford.

"I don't know yet. Mannering has already urged me to consult Scotland Yard at once. Indeed, he was going to approach them to-day. Mr. Hardcastle shall certainly be invited to do what he can. I shall leave no stone unturned to reach the truth. Yet what even such a man can do is difficult to see. The walls of the Grey Room are solid, the floor is of sound oak, the ceiling is nine or ten inches thick, and supported by immense beams. The hearth is modern, and the chimney not large enough to admit a human being. This was proved twelve years ago."

"Give him a free hand all the same—with servants and every-body. I should ask him to come as your guest, then nobody need know who he is, and he can pursue his investigations the more freely."

Felix Fayre-Michell made this suggestion after luncheon was ended, and Masters and Fred Caunter had left the room. Then the conversation showed signs of drifting back to sentimentality. Sir Walter saw it coming in their eyes, and sought to head them off by inquiring concerning their own movements.

"Can I be of any service to simplify your plans? I fear this terrible event has put you all to great inconvenience."

"Our inconvenience is nothing beside your sorrow, dear Walter," said Nelly Travers.

All declared that if they could serve the cause in any way they would gladly stop at Chadlands, but since they were powerless to assist, they felt that the sooner they departed the better.

"We go, but we leave our undying sympathy and commiseration, dear friend," declared Mr. Travers. "Believe me, this has aged my wife and myself. Probably it would not be an exaggeration to say it has aged us all. That he should have come through Jutland, done worthy deeds, won honorable mention and the D. S. O., then to be snatched out of life in this incomprehensible manner—nay, perhaps even by supernatural means, for we cannot yet actually declare it is not so. All this makes it impossible to say much that can comfort you or dear Mary. Time must pass I fear, Walter. You must get her away into another environment. Thank Heaven she has youth on her side."

"Yes, yes, I shall live for her, be sure of that." He left them and presently spoke to his nephew alone in his study.

"Do what you can for them. Handford and Vane are getting off this afternoon, the rest early to-morrow. I don't think I shall be able to dine with them to-night. Tom's father will be here. I fear he is likely to be prostrated when he knows that all is over."

"No, he's not that kind of man, uncle. Mary tells me he will want to get to the bottom of this in his own way. He's one of the fighting sort, but he believes in a lot of queer things. I'm going in to Newton with Colonel Vane, and shall meet Mannering there about—about Sir Howard Fellowes. He'll come down to-morrow, no doubt, perhaps to-night. Mannering will know."

"And tell Mannering to insist on a detective called Peter Hardcastle for the inquiry. If he's left Scotland Yard and acting independently, none the less engage him. I shall, of course, thankfully pay anything to get this tragedy explained."

"Be sure they will explain it."

"If they do not I shall be tempted to leave altogether. Indeed, I may do so in any case. Mary will never reconcile herself to live here now."

"Don't bother about the future, don't think about it. Consider yourself, and take a little rest this afternoon. Everybody is very concerned for you, they mean to be awfully decent in their way; but I know how they try you. They can't help it. Such a thing takes them out of their daily round, and beggars their experience, and makes them excited and tactless. There's no precedent for them, and you know how most people depend on precedent and how they're bowled over before anything new."

"I will go to Mary, I think. Has the undertaker been?"

"Yes, uncle."

"I want him to be buried with us here. I should not suppose his father will object."

"Not likely. Mary would wish it so."

"It was so typical of Mary to think of Septimus May before everybody. She put her own feelings from her that she might soften the blow for him."

"She would."

"Are you equal to telling the clergyman at the station that his son is dead, or can't you trust yourself to do it?"

"I expect he'll know it well enough, but I'll tell him everything there is to tell. I remember long ago, after the wedding, that he was interested in haunted rooms, and said he believed in such things on Scriptural grounds."

Sir Walter took pause at this statement.

"That is news to me. Supposing he—However, we need not trouble ourselves with him yet. He will, of course, be as deeply concerned to get to the bottom of this as I am, though we must not interfere, or make the inquiry harder for Hardcastle than he is bound to find it."

"Certainly nobody must interfere. I only hope we can get Peter Hardcastle."

"Tell them to call me when Mr. May arrives, and not sooner. I'll see Mary, then lie down for an hour or two."

"You feel all right? Should you care to see Mannering?"

"I am right enough. Say 'Good-bye' to Vane and Miles Handford for me. They may have to return here presently. One can't tell who may be wanted, and who may not be. I don't know—these things are outside my experience; but they had better both leave you their directions."

"I'll ask them."

Sir Walter visited his daughter, and changed his mind about sleeping. She was passing through an hour of unspeakable horror. The dark temple of realization had opened for her and she was treading its dreary aisles. Henceforth for long days— she told herself for ever—sorrow and sense of unutterable loss must be her companions and share her waking hours.

They stopped together alone till the dusk came down and Mannering returned. He stayed but a few minutes, and presently they heard his car start again, while that containing the departing guests and Henry Lennox immediately followed it.

In due course Septimus May returned to Chadlands with him. The clergyman had heard of his son's end, and went immediately to see the dead man. There Mary joined him, and witnessed his self-control under very shattering grief. He was thin, clean-shaven—a grey man with smouldering eyes and an expression of endurance. A fanatic in faith, by virtue of certain asperities of mind and a critical temperament, he had never made friends, won his parish into close ties, nor advanced the cause of his religion as he had yearned to do. With the zeal of a reformer, he had entered the ministry in youth; but while commanding respect for his own rule of conduct and the example he set his little flock, their affection he never won. The people feared him, and dreaded his stern criticism. Once certain spirits, smarting under pulpit censure, had sought to be rid of him; but no grounds existed on which they could eject the reverend gentleman or challenge his status. He remained, therefore, as many like him remain, embedded in his parish and unknown beyond it. He was a poor student of human nature and life had dimmed his old ambitions, soured his hopes; but it had not clouded his faith. With a passionate fervor he believed all that he tried to teach, and held that an almighty, all loving and all merciful God controlled every destiny, ordered existence for the greatest and least, and allowed nothing to happen upon earth that was not the best that could happen for the immortal beings He had created in His own image. Upon this assurance fell the greatest, almost the only, blow that life could deal Septimus May. He was stricken suddenly, fearfully with his unutterable loss; but his agony turned into prayer while he knelt beside his son. He prayed with a fiery intensity and a resonant vibration of voice that scorched rather than comforted the woman who knelt beside him. The fervor of the man's emotion and the depth of his conviction, running like a torrent through the narrow channels of his understanding, were destined presently to complicate a situation sufficiently painful without intervention; for a time swiftly came when Septimus May forced his beliefs upon Chadlands and opposed them to the opinions of other people as deeply concerned as himself to explain the death of his son.

Mr. May, learning that most of the house party could not depart until the following morning, absented himself from dinner; indeed, he spent his time almost entirely with his boy, and when night came kept vigil beside him. Something of the strange possession of his mind already appeared, in curious hints that puzzled Sir Walter; but it was not until after the post-mortem examination and inquest that his extraordinary views were elaborated.

Millicent Fayre-Michell and her uncle were the first to depart on the following day. The girl harbored a grievance.

"Surely Mary might have seen me a moment to say 'Good-bye,'" she said. "It's a very dreadful thing, but we've been so sympathetic and understanding about it that I think they ought to feel rather grateful. They might realize how trying it is for us, too. And to let me go without even seeing her—she saw Mrs. Travers over and over again."

"Do not mind. Grief makes people selfish," declared Felix. "Probably we should not have acted so. I think we should have hidden our sufferings and faced our duty; but perhaps we are exceptional. I dare say Mrs. May will write and express regret and gratitude later. We must allow for her youth and sorrow."

Mr. Fayre-Michell rather prided himself on the charity of this conclusion.

When Mr. and Mrs. Travers departed, Sir Walter bade them

farewell. The lady wept, and her tears fell on his hand as he held it. She was hysterical.

"For Heaven's sake don't let Mary be haunted by that dreadful priest," she said. "There is something terrible about him. He has no bowels of compassion. I tried to console him for the loss of his son, and he turned upon me as if I were weak-minded."

"I had to tell him he was being rude and forgetting that he spoke to a lady," said Ernest Travers. "One makes every allowance for a father's sufferings; but they should not take the form of abrupt and harsh speech to a sympathetic fellow-creature—nay, to anyone, let alone a woman. His sacred calling ought to—"

"A man's profession cannot alter his manners, my dear Ernest; they come from defects of temperament, no doubt. May must not be judged. His faith would move mountains."

"So would mine," said Ernest Travers, "and so would yours, Walter. But it is perfectly possible to be a Christian and a gentleman. To imply that our faith was weak because we expressed ordinary human emotions and pitied him unfeignedly for the loss of his only child—"

"Good-bye, good-bye, my dear friends," answered the other. "I cannot say how I esteem your kindly offices in this affliction. May we meet again presently. God bless and keep you both."

The post-mortem examination revealed no physical reason why Thomas May should have ceased to breathe. Neither did the subsequent investigations of a Government analytical chemist throw any light upon the sailor's sudden death. No cause existed, and therefore none could be reported at the inquest held a day later.

The coroner's jury brought in a verdict rarely heard, but none dissented from it. They held that May had received his death "by the hand of God."

"All men receive death from the hand of God," said Septimus

May, when the judicial inquiry was ended. "They receive life from the hand of God also. But, while bowing to that, there is a great deal more we are called to do when God's hand falls as it has fallen upon my son. To-night I shall pray beside his dust, and presently, when he is at peace, I shall be guided. There is a grave duty beside me, Sir Walter, and none must come between me and that duty."

"There is a duty before all of us, and be sure nobody will shrink from it. I have done what is right, so far. We have secured a famous detective—the most famous in England, they tell me. He is called Peter Hardcastle, and he will, I hope, be able to arrive here immediately."

The clergyman shook his head.

"I will say nothing at present," he answered. "But, believe me, a thousand detectives cannot explain my son's death. I shall return to this subject after the funeral, Sir Walter. But my conviction grows that the reason of these things will never be revealed to the eye of science. To the eye of faith alone we must trust the explanation of what has happened. There are things concealed from the wise and prudent—to be revealed unto babes."

That night the master of Chadlands, his nephew, and the priest dined together, and Henry Lennox implored a privilege.

"I feel I owe it to poor Tom in a way," he said. "I beg that you will let me spend the night in the Grey Room, Uncle Walter. I would give my soul to clear this."

But his uncle refused with a curt shake of the head, and the clergyman uttered a reproof.

"Do not speak so lightly," he said. "You use a common phrase and a very objectionable phrase, young man. Do you rate your soul so low that you would surrender it for the satisfaction of a morbid craving? For that is all this amounts to. Not to such an inquirer will my son's death reveal its secret."

"I have already received half-a-dozen letters from people offering and wishing to spend a night in that accursed room," said Sir Walter.

"Do not call it 'accursed' until you know more," urged Septimus May.

"You have indeed charity," answered the other.

"Why withhold charity? We must approach the subject in the only spirit that can disarm the danger. These inquirers who seek to solve the mystery are not concerned with my son's death, only the means that brought it about. Not to such as they will any answer be vouchsafed, and not to the spirit of materialistic inquiry, either. I speak what I know, and will say more upon the subject at another time."

"You cannot accept this awful thing without resentment or demur, Mr. May?" asked Henry Lennox.

"Who shall demur? Did not even the unenlightened men who formed the coroner's jury declare that Tom passed into another world by the hand of God? Can we question our Creator? I, too, desire as much as any human being can an explanation; what is more, I am far more confident of an explanation than you or any other man. But that is because I already know the only road by which it will please God to send an explanation. And that is not the road which scientists or rationalists are used to travel. It is a road that I must be allowed to walk alone."

He left them after dinner, and returned to his daughter-in-law. She had determined not to attend the funeral, but Mr. May argued with her, examined her reasons, found them, in his opinion, not sufficient, and prevailed with her to change her mind.

"Drink the cup to the dregs," he said. "This is our grief, our trial. None feel and know what we feel and know, and your youth is called to bear a burden heavy to be borne. You must stand beside his grave as surely as I must commit him to it."

Men will go far to look upon the coffin of one whose end happens to be mysterious or terrible. The death of Sir Walter's son-in-law had made much matter for the newspapers, and not only Chadlands, but the countryside converged upon the naval funeral, lined the route to the grave, and crowded the little burying ground where the dead man would lie. Cameras pointed their eyes at the gun-carriage and the mourners behind it. The photographers worked for a sort of illustrated paper that tramples with a swine's hoofs and routs up with a swine's nose the matter its clients best love to purchase. Mary, supported by her father and her cousin, preserved a brave composure. Indeed, she was less visibly moved than they. It seemed that the ascetic parent of the dead had power to lift the widow to his own stern self-control. The chaplain of Tom May's ship assisted at the service, but Septimus May conducted it. Not a few old messmates attended, for the sailor had been popular, and his unexpected death brought genuine grief to many men. Under a pile of flowers the coffin was carried to the grave. Rare and precious blossoms came from Sir Walter's friends, and H. M. S. Indomitable sent a mighty anchor of purple violets. Mr. May read the service without a tremor, but his eyes blazed out of his lean head, and there lacked not other signs to indicate the depth of emotion he concealed. Then the bluejackets who had drawn the gun-carriage fired a volley, and the rattle of their musketry echoed sharply from the church tower.

Upon the evening of the day that followed Septimus May resumed the subject concerning which he had already fitfully spoken. His ideas were now in order, and he brought a formidable argument to support a strange request. Indeed, it amounted to a demand, and for a time it seemed doubtful whether Sir Walter would deny him. The priest, indeed, declared that he could take no denial, and his host was thankful that other and stronger arguments than his own were at hand to argue the other side. For Dr. Mannering stayed at the manor house after the funeral, and the Rev. Noel Prodgers, the vicar of Chadlands, a distant connection of the Lennoxes, was also dining there. Until now Mannering could not well speak, but he invited himself to dinner on the day after the funeral that he might press a course of action upon those who had suffered so severely. He wished Sir Walter to take his daughter away at once, for her health's sake, and while advancing this advice considered the elder also, for these things had upset the master of Chadlands in mind and body, and Mannering was aware of it.

On the morrow Peter Hardcastle would arrive, and he had urgently directed that his coming should be in a private capacity, unknown to the local police or neighborhood. Neither did he wish the staff of Chadlands to associate him with the tragedy.

An official examination of the room had been made by the local constabulary, as upon the occasion of Nurse Forrester's death; but it was a perfunctory matter, and those responsible for it understood that special attention would presently be paid to the problem by the supreme authority.

"After this man has been and gone, I do earnestly beg you to leave England and get abroad, Sir Walter," said Mannering. "I think it your duty, not only for your girl's sake, but your own. Do not even wait for the report. There is nothing to keep you, and I shall personally be very thankful and relieved if you will manage this and take Mary to some fresh scenes, a place or country that she has not visited before. There is nothing like an entirely novel environment for distracting the mind, bracing the nerves, and restoring tone."

"I must do my duty," answered the other, "and that remains to be seen. If Hardcastle should find out anything, there may be a call upon me. At least, I cannot turn my back upon Chadlands till the mystery is threshed out to the bottom, as far as man can do it."

It was then that Septimus May spoke and astounded his hearers.

"You give me the opportunity to introduce my subject," he said, "for it bears directly on Sir Walter's intentions, and it is in my power, as I devoutly believe, to free him swiftly of any further need to remain here. I am, of course, prepared to argue for my purpose, but would rather not do so. Briefly, I hold it a vital obligation to spend this night in the Grey Room, and I ask that no obstacle of any kind be raised to prevent my doing so. The wisdom of man is foolishness before the wit of God, and what I desire to do is God's will and wish, impressed upon me while I knelt for long hours and prayed to know it. I am convinced, and that should be enough. In this matter I am far from satisfied that all has yet been done, within the Almighty's purpose and direction, to discover the mystery of our terrible loss. But He helps those who help themselves, remember, and I owe it to my son, Sir Walter, and you owe it to your daughter Mary first, and the community also, to take such steps as Heaven, through me, has now directed."

They were for a moment struck dumb by this extraordinary assertion and demand. A thousand objections leaped to the lips of the elder men, and Mr. Prodgers, a devout young Christian of poor physique but great spiritual courage, found himself as interested by this fearless demand of faith as the others were alarmed by it.

Sir Walter spoke.

"We know it is so, May. None recognizes our obligations, both to the living and the dead, more acutely than I do. A very famous man of European reputation will be here to-morrow, and if you, too, desire a representative, you have only got to say so."

"I desire no representative armed with material craft or knowledge of criminal procedure. I am my own representative, and I come armed with greater power than any you can command on earth, Sir Walter. I mean my Maker's response to my prayer. I must spend the night in that room, and cannot leave Chadlands until I have done so. I trust to no human expedient or precaution, for such things would actually disarm me; but my faith is in the God I have served to the best of my power from my youth up. I entertain not the least shadow of fear or doubt. To fear or doubt would be to fail. I rely absolutely on the Supreme Being who has permitted this unspeakable sorrow to fall upon us, and there is no living man less likely than myself to fall a victim to the unknown spirit hidden here and permitted to exercise such awful control over us. The time has come to challenge that spirit in the name of its Maker, and to cleanse your house once and for all of something which, potent for evil though it is allowed to be, must yield to the forces of the Most High, even in the feeble hand of His minister."

The doctor spoke.

"Is it possible, sir, that you attribute your son's death to anything but natural physical forces?" he asked.

"Is it possible to do otherwise? How can you, of all men, ask? Science has spoken—or, rather, science has been struck dumb. No natural, physical force is responsible for his end. He died without any cause that you could discover. This is no new thing, however. History records that men have passed similarly under visitations beyond human power to explain. If the Lord could slay multitudes in a night at a breath, as we know from the pages of the Old Testament, then it is certain He can still end the life of any man at any moment, and send His messengers to do so. I believe in good and evil spirits as I believe in my Bible, and I know that, strong and terrible though they may be and gifted with capital powers against our flesh, yet the will of God is stronger than the strongest of them. These things, I say, have happened before. They are sent to try our faith. I do not mourn my son, save with the blind, natural pang of paternity, because I know that he has been withdrawn from this world for higher purposes in another; but the means of his going I demand to investigate, because they may signify much more than his death itself. One reason for his death may be this: that we are now called to understand what is hidden in the Grey Room. My son's death may have been necessary to that explanation. Human intervention may be demanded there. One of God's immortal souls, for reasons we cannot tell, may be chained in that room, waiting its liberation at human hands. We are challenged, and I accept the challenge, being impelled thereto by the sacred message that has been put into my heart."

Even his fellow-priest stared in bewilderment at Septimus May's extraordinary opinions, while to the physician this was the chatter of a lunatic.

"I will take my Bible into that haunted room to-night," concluded the clergyman, "and I will pray to God, Who sits above both quick and dead, to protect me, guide me, and lead me to my duty."

Sir Walter spoke.

"You flout reason when you say these things, my dear May."

"And why should I not flout reason? What Christian but knows well enough that reason is the staff that breaks in our hands and wounds us? Much of our most vital experience has no part nor lot with reason. A thousand things happen in the soul's history which reason cannot account for. A thousand moods, temptations, incitements prompt us to action or deter us from it—urge us to do or avoid—for which reason is not responsible. Reason, if we bring these emotions to it, cannot even pronounce upon them. Yet in them and from them springs the life of the soul and the conviction of immortality. 'To act on impulse'—who but daily realizes that commonplace in his own experience? The mind does not only play tricks and laugh at reason in dreams while we sleep. It laughs at reason while we wake, and the sanest spirit experiences inspired moments, mad moments, unaccountable impulses the reason for which he knows not. The ancients explained these as temptations of malicious and malignant spirits or promptings from unseen beings who wish man well. And where the urge is to evil, that may well be the truth; and where it is to good, who can doubt whence the inspiration comes?"

"And shall not my inspiration—to employ the cleverest detective in England—be also of good?" asked Sir Walter.

"Emphatically not. Because this thing is in another category than that of human crime. It is lifted upon a plane where the knowledge of man avails nothing. You are a Christian, and you should understand this as well as I do. If there is danger, then I am secure, because I have the only arms that can avail in a battle of the spirit. My trust is shield enough against any evil being that may roam this earth or be held by invisible bonds within the walls of the Grey Room. I will justify the ways of God to man and, through the channel of potent prayer, exorcise this presence and bring peace to your afflicted house. For any living fellow-creature would I gladly pit my faith against evil; how much more, then, in a matter where my very own life's blood has been shed? You cannot deny me this. It is my right."

"I will ask you to listen to the arguments against you, nevertheless," replied Mannering. "You have propounded an extraordinary theory, and must not mind if we disagree with you."

"Speak for yourself alone, then," answered May. "I do not ask or expect a man of your profession to agree with me. But the question ceases to be your province."

"Do not say that, sir," urged Henry Lennox. "I don't think my uncle agrees with you either. You are assuming too much."

"Honestly, I can't quite admit your assumption, my dear May," declared Sir Walter. "You go too far—farther than is justified at this stage of events, at any rate. Were we in no doubt that a spirit is granted power within my house to destroy human life, then I confess, with due precautions, I could not deny you access to it in the omnipotent Name you invoke. I am a Christian and believe my Bible as soundly as you do. But why assume such an extraordinary situation? Why seek a supernatural cause for dear Tom's death before we are satisfied that no other exists?"

"Are you not satisfied? What mortal man can explain the facts on any foundation of human knowledge?"

"Consider how limited human knowledge is," said Mannering, "and grant that we have not exhausted its possibilities yet. There may be some physical peculiarity about the room, some deadly but perfectly natural chemical accident, some volatile stuff, in roof or walls, that reacts to the lowered temperatures of night. A thousand rare chance combinations of matter may occur which are capable of examination, and which, under skilled experiment, will resolve their secret. Nothing it more bewildering than a good conjuring trick till we know how it is done, and Nature is the supreme conjurer. We have not found out all her tricks, and never shall do so; but we very well know that a solution to all of them exists."

"A material outlook and arrogant," said the priest.

Whereupon Mannering grew a little warm.

"It is neither material nor arrogant. I am humbler than you, and your positive assertion seems much the more arrogant. This is the twentieth century, and your mediaeval attitude would win no possible sympathy or support from any educated man."

"Truth can afford to be patient," answered May. "But I, too, am quite sane, though your face doubts it. I do not claim that human prayer can alter physical laws, and I do not ask my Maker to work a miracle on my behalf or suspend the operations of cause and effect. But I am satisfied that we are in a region outside our experience and on another plane and dimension than those controlled by natural law. God has permitted us to enter such a region. He has opened the door into this mystery. He has spoken to my soul and so directed me that I cannot sit with folded hands. This is, I repeat, a challenge to me personally.

"There is, as I potently believe, a being in bondage here which only the voice of God, speaking through one of His creatures, can liberate. If I am wrong, then I shall pray in vain; if right, as I know by deepest conviction and intuition, then my prayer must avail. In any case, I do my duty, and if I myself was called to die while so doing, what nobler death can I desire?"

Mannering regarded the speaker with growing concern. But he still assumed sanity on the part of the reverend gentleman, and still felt considerable irritation mix with his solicitude.

"You must consider others a little," he said.

"No, Dr. Mannering; they must consider me. Providence sends me a message denied to the rest of you, because I am a fit recipient; you are not. It is Newman's 'Illative Sense'—a conviction arising from well-springs far deeper and purer than those that account for human reason. I know because I know. Reasoning, at best, is mere inference deduced from observation, but I am concerned with an inspiration—a something akin to the gift of prophecy."

"Then I can only hope that Sir Walter will exercise his rights and responsibilities and deny you what you wish."

"He has faith, and I am sorry that you lack it."

"No, Mr. May, you must not say that. It is entirely reason-able that Mannering should ask you to consider others," said Sir Walter. "To you a sudden and peaceful death might be no ill; but it would be a very serious ill to the living—a loss to your work on earth, which is not done, a shock and grief to those who respect you, and a reflection on all here."

"Let the living minister to the living and put their trust in God."

Mannering spoke to the vicar of Chadlands.

"What do you think, Prodgers? You are a parson, too, yet may be able to see with our eyes. Surely common sense shouldn't be left out of our calculations, even if they concern the next world?"

"I respect Mr. May's faith," answered the younger priest, "and assuredly I believe that if we eliminate all physical and natural causes from poor Captain May's death, then no member of our sacred calling should fear to spend the night alone in that room. Jacob wrestled with the angel of light. Shall the servants of God fear to oppose a dark angel?"

"Well spoken," said Mr. May.

"But that is not all, sir," continued Noel Prodgers. "It is impossible that we can share such certainty as you claim. Probability lies entirely against it. This has happened twice, remember, and each time a valuable and precious life disap-pears, for causes beyond our knowledge. That, however, is no reason for assuming the causes are beyond all human knowl-edge. We do not all possess learning in physics. I would venture most earnestly to beg you to desist, at least until much more has been done and this famous professional man has made such researches as his genius suggests. That is only reasonable, and reason, after all, is a mighty gift of God—a gift, no doubt, often abused by finite beings, who actually use it to defy the Giver—yet none the less, in its proper place, the handmaid of faith and the light of true progress."

But Septimus May argued against him. "To shelter behind reason at such a moment is to blunt the sword of the spirit," he replied, "and human reason is never the handmaid of faith, as you wrongly suggest, but her obdurate, unsleeping foe. That which metaphysicians call intuition, and which I call the voice of God, tells me in clear tones that my boy died by no human agency whatever and by no natural accident. He was wrapt from this life to the next in the twinkling of an eye by forces, or a force, concerning which we know nothing save through the Word of God. I will go farther. I will venture to declare that this death-dealing ghost, or discarnate but conscious being, may not be, as you say, a dark angel—perhaps not wholly evil—perhaps not evil at all. One thing none can question—it did the will of its Creator, as we all must, and we are not, therefore, justified in asserting that a malignant force was exerted. To say so is to speak in terms of our own bitter loss and our own aching hearts. But we are justified in believing that a fearful, unknown power was liberated during the night that Tom died, and I desire to approach that power upon my knees and with my life in my Maker's hands."

The conviction of this righteous but superstitious soul was uttered with passionate zeal. He puzzled to understand how fellow Christians could argue against him, and much resented the fact that Sir Walter withstood his claim and declined to permit the experiment he desired to make. A formalist and precisian, he held any sort of doubt to be backsliding before the message in his own heart. They argued unavailingly with him, and Henry Lennox suggested a compromise.

"Why is it vital, after all, that only one should undertake this ordeal?" he asked. "I begged you to let me try—for revenge."

"Do not use that word," said Mr. Prodgers.

"Well, at any rate, I feel just as great a call to be there as Tom's father can feel—just as pressing a demand and desire. There may have been foul play. At any rate, the thing was done by an active agency, and Tom was taken in some way at a disadvantage. There was no fair fight, I'll swear. He was evidently kneeling, calmly enough looking out of the window, when he died, and the blow must have been a coward's blow, struck from behind, whoever struck it."

"There was no blow, Henry," said Sir Walter.

"Death is a blow, uncle—the most awful blow a strong man can be called to suffer, surely. And I beg this, that if you won't let me face the infernal thing alone you'll let me share this business with Mr. May. He can pray and I can—watch."

But the dead man's father made short work of Henry's proposition.

"You are introducing that very element of rationalism to be, before all things, distrusted here. The mere introduction of human precaution and human weapons would sully faith and make of no avail the only sure means of winning light on this solemn problem. Reason, so employed, would be a hindrance—an actual danger. Only absolute faith can unravel the mystery before us."

"Then, frankly, I tell you that I lack any such absolute faith," declared Sir Walter.

"Do not say that—you libel yourself and are letting a base and material fear cloud your own trust," answered May. "As there is no human reason for what has happened, so no human reason will be found to explain it. By denying me, you are denying the sole means by which this dark terror can be banished. You are denying God's offer of peace. We must not only seek peace, but ensure it. That means that we are now called to take such steps as the Almighty puts at our service by the road of conscience and faith. I have a right to this revelation as my boy's father. The cup is mine, and you will do very wrongly if you deny me the right to drink it. I desire to say, 'Peace be to this house' before I leave it, and, Christian to Christian, you cannot deny me, or hesitate as to your answer."

No argument would bend his obstinate conviction, and he debated with great force from his own standpoint. He presented a man overmastered and mentally incapable of appreciating any argument against his possession.

But Sir Walter, now determined, was as obstinate as the clergyman. Mannering bluntly declared that it would be suicide on May's part, and a conniving at the same by any who permitted him to attempt his vigil.

"I, too, must do my duty as I see it," summed up the master of Chadlands, "and after I have done so, then we may be in a position to admit the case is altered."

The other suddenly rose and lifted his hands. He was trembling with emotion.

"May my God give a sign, then!" he cried.

They were silent a moment, for courtesy or astonishment. Nothing happened, and presently Sir Walter spoke:

"You must bear with me. You are upset, and scarcely know the gravity of the things you say. To-morrow the physical and material investigation that I consider proper, and the world has a right to demand, will be made—in a spirit, I hope, as earnest and devout as your own. And if after that no shadow of explanation is forthcoming, and no peril to life can be discovered, then I should feel disposed to consider your views more seriously—with many reserves, however. At any rate, it will be your turn then, if you still adhere to your opinions; and I am sure all just persons who hear of your purpose would join their prayers with you."

"Your faith is weak, though you believe it strong," answered the other.

And he was equally curt when the physician advised him to take a sleeping-draught before retiring. He bade them "Good-night" without more words, and went to his room, while after further conversation, Dr. Mannering and Mr. Prodgers took their leave.

The former strongly urged Sir Walter to set some sort of guard outside the door of the Grey Room.

"That man's not wholly sane to-night," he declared, "and he appears to glory in the fact that he isn't. He must surely be aware that much he said was superstitious bosh. Look after him. Guard his own apartment. That will be the simplest plan."

When they had gone, Sir Walter addressed his nephew. They went upstairs together and stood for a moment outside the Grey Room. The door was wide open, and the place brilliantly lighted by a high-powered bulb. So had it been by night ever since the disaster. None of the household entered it, and none, save Sir Walter or Henry, was willing to do so until more should be known.

"I have your word of honor you will not go into that room to-night," said his uncle; "but such is the mental condition of this poor clergyman that I can but feel Mannering is right. May might, from some fancied call of the spirit, take the law into his own hands and do what he wishes to do. This must be prevented at any cost. I will ask you, Henry, to follow the doctor's suggestion on my behalf, and keep guard over him. Oppose him actively if he should appear, and call me. I would suggest that Caunter or Masters accompanied you, but that is only to make gossip and mystery."

"On no account. I'll look after him. You can trust me. I expect he's pretty worn out after such a harrowing day, poor old beggar. He'll probably sleep soundly enough when he gets to bed."

"I trust so. I cannot offer to aid you myself, for I am dead beat," said the other.

Then they parted, and the younger presently took up a position in the west wing of the house, where Septimus May had his bedroom.

Not until sunrise did Henry Lennox go to his own chamber, but his sleepless night proved a needless precaution, for Septimus May gave no sign.

CHAPTER V.

THE UNSEEN MOVES

Before ten o'clock on the following morning Peter Hardcastle, who had travelled by the night train from Paddington, was at Chadlands. A car had gone into Newton Abbot to meet him, as no train ran on the branch line until a later hour.

The history of the detective was one of hard work, crowned at last by a very remarkable success. His opportunity had come, and he had grasped it. The accident of the war and the immense publicity given to his capture of a German secret agent had brought him into fame, and raised him to the heights of his profession. Moreover, the extraordinary histrionic means taken to achieve his purpose, and the picturesqueness of the details, captured that latent love of romance common to all minds. Hardcastle had become a lion; women were foolish about him; he might have made a great match and retired into private life had he desired to do so. At the present time an American heiress ardently wished to wed the man.

But he was not fond of women, and only in love with his

business. A hard life in the seamy places of the world had made him something of a cynic. He had always appreciated his own singular powers, and consciousness of ability, combined with a steadfast patience and unconquerable devotion to his "art," as he called it, had brought him through twenty years in the police force. He began at the bottom and reached the top. He was the son of a small shopkeeper, and now that his father was dead his mother still ran a little eating-house for her own satisfaction and occupation.

Peter Hardcastle was forty. He had already made arrangements to leave Scotland Yard and set up, single-handed, as a private inquiry agent. The mystery of Chadlands would be the last case to occupy him as a Government servant. In a measure he regretted the fact, for the death of Captain Thomas May, concerning which every known particular was now in his possession, attracted him, and he knew the incident had been widely published. It was a popular mystery, and, as a man of business, he well understood the professional value of such sensations to the man who resolves the puzzle. His attitude toward the case appeared at the outset, and Sir Walter, who had been deeply impressed by the opinions of the dead man's father, and even unconsciously influenced by them, now found himself in the presence of a very different intellect. There was nothing in the least superstitious about Peter Hardcastle. He uttered the views of a remorseless realist, and at the outset committed himself to certain definite assumptions. The inhabitants of the manor house were informed that a friend of Sir Walter's had come to visit Chadlands, and they saw nothing to make them doubt it. For Peter was a great actor. He had mixed with all classes, and the detective had the imitative cleverness to adapt himself in speech and attire to every society. He even claimed that he could think with the brains of anybody and adapt his inner mind, as well as his outer shape, to the changing environment of his activities. He appreciated the histrionics that operate out of sight, and would adopt the blank purview of the ignorant, the deeper attitude of the cultured, or the solid posture of that class whose education and inherent opinions is based upon tradition. He had made a study of the superficial etiquette and manners and customs of what is called "the best" society, and knew its ways as a naturalist patiently masters the habits of a species.

Chadlands saw a small, fair man with scanty hair, a clean-shaven face, a rather feminine cast of features, a broad forehead, slate-grey eyes, and a narrow, lipless mouth which revealed very fine white teeth when he spoke. It was a colorless face and challenged no attention; but it was a face that served as an excellent canvas, and few professional actors had ever surpassed Peter in the art of making up their features.

Similarly he could disguise his voice, the natural tones of which were low, monotonous, and of no arrestive quality. Mr. Hardcastle surprised Sir Walter by his commonplace appearance and seeming youth, for he looked ten years younger than the forty he had lived. A being so undistinguished rather disappointed his elder, for the master of Chadlands had imagined that any man of such wide celebrity must offer superficial marks of greatness.

But here was one so insignificant and so undersized that it seemed impossible to imagine him a famous Englishman. His very voice, in its level, matter-of-fact tones, added to the suggestion of mediocrity.

Sir Walter found, however, that the detective did not undervalue himself. He was not arrogant, but revealed decision and immense will power. From the first he imposed his personality, and made people forget the accidents of his physical constitution. He said very little during breakfast, but listened with attention to the conversation.

He observed that Henry Lennox spoke seldom, but studied him unobtrusively, as a man concerning whom he specially desired to know more. Hardcastle proved himself well educated; indeed, his reading, studiously pursued, and his intellectual attainments, developed by hard work and ambition, far exceeded those of any present.

The clergyman returned to his own ground, and expressed his former opinions, to which Hardcastle listened without a shadow of the secret surprise they awoke in him.

"The Witchcraft Act assumes that there can be no possible communication between living men and spirits," he said in answer to an assertion; whereon Septimus May instantly took up the challenge.

"A fatuous, archaic assumption, and long since destroyed by actual, human experience," he replied. "It is time such blasphemous folly should be banished from the Statute Book. I say 'blasphemous' because such an Act takes no cognizance of the Word of God. Outworn Acts of Parliament are responsible for a great deal of needless misery in this world, and it is high time these ordinances of another generation were sent to the dust heap."

"In that last opinion I heartily agree with you," declared the detective.

Henry ventured a quotation. He was much interested to learn whether Hardcastle had any views on the ghost theory.

"Goethe says that matter cannot exist without spirit, or spirit without matter. Would you sub-scribe to that, Mr. Hardcastle?"

"Partially. Matter can exist without spirit, which you may prove by getting under an avalanche; but I do most emphatically agree that spirit cannot exist without matter. 'Divorced from matter, where is life?' asks Tyndall, and nobody can answer him."

"You misunderstand Goethe," declared Mr. May. "In metaphysics—"

"I have no use for metaphysics. Believe me, the solemn humbug of metaphysics doesn't take in a policeman for a moment. Juggling with words never advanced the world's welfare or helped the cause of truth. What, for any practical purpose, does it matter how subjectively true a statement may be if it is objectively false? Life is just as real as I am myself—no more and no less—and all the metaphysical jargon in the world won't prevent my shins from bleeding wet, red blood when I bark them against a stone."

"You don't believe in the supernatural then?" asked Mr. May.

"Most emphatically not."

"How extraordinary! And how, if I may ask, do you fill the terrible vacuum in your life that such a denial must create?"

"I have never been conscious of such a vacuum. I was a sceptic from my youth up. No doubt those who were nurtured in superstition, when reason at last conquers and they break away, may experience a temporary blank; but the wonders of nature and the achievements of man and the demands of the suffering world—these should be enough to fill any blank for a reasonable creature."

"If such are your opinions, you will fail here," declared the clergyman positively.

"Why do you feel so sure of that?"

"Because you are faced with facts that have no material explanation. They are supernatural, or supernormal, if you prefer the word."

"'One world at a time,' is a very good motto in my judgment," replied Hardcastle. "We will exhaust the possibilities of this world first, sir."

"They have already been exhausted. Only a simple, straight-forward question awaits your reply. Do you believe in another world or do you not?"

"In the endless punishment or the endless happiness of men and women after they are dead?"

"If you like to confuse the issue in that way you are at liberty, of course, to do so. As a Christian, I cannot demur. The problem for the rationalist is this: How does he ignore the deeply rooted and universal conviction that there is a life to come? Is such a sanguine assurance planted in the mind of even the lowest savage for nothing? Where did the aborigines win that expectation?"

"My answer embraces the whole question from my own point of view," replied Hardcastle. "The savages got their idea of dual personality from phenomena of nature which they were unable to explain—from their dreams, from their own shadows on the earth and reflections in water, from the stroke of the lightning and the crash of the thunder, from the echo of their own voices, thrown back to them from crags and cliffs. These things created their superstitions. Ignorance bred terror, and terror bred gods and demons—first out of the forces of nature. That is the appalling mental legacy handed down in varying shapes to all the children of men. We labor under them to this day."

"You would dare to say our most sacred verities have sprung from the dreams of savages?"

Hardcastle smiled.

"It is true. And dreams, we further know, are often the result of indigestion. Early man didn't understand the art of cookery, and therefore no doubt his stomach had a great deal to put up with. We have to thank his bear steaks and wolf chops for a great deal of our cherished nonsense, no doubt."

Sir Walter, marking the clergyman's flashing eyes, changed

the subject, and Septimus May, who observed his concern, restrained a bitter answer. But he despaired of the detective from that moment, and proposed to himself a future assault on such detested modern opinions when opportunity occurred.

After breakfast Mr. Hardcastle begged for a private interview with the master of Chadlands, and for two hours sat in his study and took him through the case from the beginning.

He put various questions concerning the members of the recent house party, and presently begged that Henry Lennox might join them.

"I should like to hear the account of what passed on the night between him and Captain May," he said.

Henry joined them, and detailed his experience. While he talked, Hardcastle appraised him, and perceived that certain nebulous opinions, which had begun to crystallize in his own mind, could have no real foundation. The detective believed that he was confronted with a common murder, and on hearing Henry's history, as part of Sir Walter's story with the rest, perceived that the old lover of Mary Lennox had last seen her husband alive, had drunk with him, and been the first to find him dead. Might not Henry have found an eastern poison in Mesopotamia? But his conversation with the young man, and the unconscious revelation of Henry himself, shattered the idea. Lennox was innocent enough.

For a moment, the information of uncle and nephew exhausted, Hardcastle returned to the matter of the breakfast discussion.

"You will, of course, understand that I am quite satisfied a material and physical explanation exists for this unfortunate event," he said. "I need hardly tell you that I am unprepared to entertain any supernatural theory of the business. I don't believe myself in ghosts, because in my experience, and it is pretty wide, ghost stories break down badly under anything like skilled and independent examination. There is a natural reason for what has happened, as there is a natural reason for everything that happens. We talk of unnatural things happening, but that is a contradiction in terms. Nothing can happen that is not natural. What we call Nature embraces every conceivable action or event or possibility. We may fail to fathom a mystery, and we know that a thousand things happen every day and night that seem beyond the power of our wits to explain; but that is only to say our wits are limited. I hold, however, that very few things happen which do not yield an explanation, sooner or later, if approached by those best trained to examine them without predisposition or prejudice. And I earnestly hope that this tragic business will give up its secret."

"May you prove the correctness of your opinions, Mr. Hardcastle," answered Sir Walter. "Would you like to see the Grey Room now?"

"I should; though I tell you frankly it is not in the Grey Room that I shall find what I seek. It does not particularly interest me, and for this reason. I do not associate Captain May's death in any way with the earlier tragedy—that of the hospital nurse, Mrs. Forrester. It is a coincidence, in my opinion, and probably, if physiology were a more perfect science than, in my experience of post-mortem examinations, it has proved to be, the reason for the lady's death would have appeared. And, for that matter, the reason for Captain May's death also. To say there was no reason is, of course, absurd. Nothing ever yet happened, or could happen, without a reason. The springs of action were arrested and the machine instantly ran down. But a man is not a clock, which can be stopped and reveal no sign of the thing that stopped it. Life is a far more complex matter than a watch-spring, and if we knew more we might not be faced with so many worthless post-mortem reports. But Sir Howard Fellowes is not often beaten. I repeat, however, I do not associate the two deaths in the Grey Room or connect them as the result of one and the same cause. I do not state this as a fact beyond dispute, but that, for the present, is my assumption. The gap in time seems too considerable. I suspect other causes, and shall have to make researches into the dead man's past life. I should wish also to examine all his property. He has been in foreign countries, and may have brought back something concerning the nature of which he was ignorant. He may possess enemies, of whom neither you nor Mrs. May have heard anything. Your knowledge of him, recollect, extends over only a short time—eight or ten months, I suppose. I shall visit his ship and his cabin in H. M. S. Indomitable also, and learn all that his fellow officers can tell me."

Sir Walter looked at his watch.

"It is now nearly one o'clock," he said, "and at two we usually take luncheon. What would you wish to do between now and then? None here but ourselves and my butler—an old friend in all my secrets—knows you have come professionally. I concealed the fact and called you 'Forbes,' at your wish, though they cannot fail to suspect, I fear."

"Thank you. I will see the room, then, and look round the place. Perhaps after luncheon, if she feels equal to the task, Mrs. May will give me a private interview. I want to learn everything possible concerning your late son-in-law—his career before Jutland, his philosophy of life, his habits and his friends."

"She will very gladly tell you everything she can."

They ascended to the Grey Room.

"Not the traditional haunt of spooks, certainly," said Peter Hardcastle as they entered the bright and cheerful chamber. The day was clear, and from the southern window unclouded sunshine came.

"Nothing is changed?" he asked.

"Nothing. The room remains as it has been for many years."

"Kindly describe exactly where Captain May was found. Perhaps Mr. Lennox will imitate his posture, if he remembers it?"

"Remember it! I shall never forget it," said Henry. "I first saw him from below. He was looking out of the open window and kneeling here on this seat."

"Let us open the window then."

The situation and attitude of the dead on discovery were imitated, and Hardcastle examined the spot. Then he himself occupied the position and looked out.

"I will ask for a ladder presently, and examine the face of the wall. Ivy, I see. Ivy has told me some very interesting secrets before to-day, Sir Walter."

"I dare say it has."

"If you will remind me at luncheon, I can tell you a truly amazing story about ivy—a story of life and death. A man could easily go and come by this window."

"Not easily I think," said Henry. "It is rather more than thirty-five feet to the ground."

"How do you know that?"

"The police, who made the original inquiry and were stopped, as you will remember, from Scotland Yard, measured it the second morning afterwards—on Monday."

"But they did not examine the face of the wall?"

"I think not. They dropped a measure from the window."

The other pursued his examination of the room. "Old furniture," he said; "very old evidently."

"It was collected in Spain by my grandfather many years ago."

"Valuable, no doubt?"

"I understand so."

"Wonderful carving. And this door?"

"It is not a door, but a cupboard in the solid wall."

Sir Walter opened the receptacle as he spoke. The cupboard—some six and a half feet high—was empty. At the back of it appeared a row of pegs for clothes.

"I can finish with the room for the present at any rate, in an hour, gentlemen," said Hardcastle. "I'll spend the time here till luncheon. Had your son-in-law any interest in old furniture, Sir Walter?"

"None whatever to my knowledge. He was interested, poor fellow, not in the contents, but in the evil reputation of the room. Its bad name dated back far beyond the occupation of my family. Captain May laughed at my mistrust, and, as you know, he came here, contrary to my express wishes, in order that he might chaff me next morning over my superstition. He wanted 'to clear its character,' as he said."

Hardcastle was turning over the stack of old oil-paintings in tarnished frames.

"Family portraits?"

"Yes."

"You mistrusted the room yourself, Sir Walter?"

"After Nurse Forrester's death I did. Not before. But while attaching no importance myself to the tradition, I respected it."

"Nobody else ever spent a night here after the lady's death?"

"Nobody. Of that I am quite certain."

"Have you not left the house since?"

"Frequently. I generally spend March, April, and May on the Continent—in France or Italy. But the house is never closed, and my people are responsible to me. The room is always locked, and when I am not in residence Abraham Masters, my butler, keeps the key. He shares my own feelings so far as the Grey Room is concerned."

The detective nodded. He was standing in the middle of the room with his hands in his pockets.

"A strange fact—the force of superstition," he said. "It seems to feed on night, where ghosts are involved. What, I suppose, credulous people call 'the powers of darkness.' But have you ever asked yourself why the spiritualists must work in the dark?"

"To simplify their operations, no doubt, and make it easier for the spirits."

"And themselves! But why is the night sacred to apparitions and supernatural phenomena generally?"

"Tradition associates them with those hours. Spiritualists say it is easier for spectres to appear in the dark by reason of their material composition. It is then that we find the most authentic accounts of their manifestations."

"Yes; because at that time human vitality is lowest and human reason weakest. Darkness itself has a curious and depressing effect on the minds of many people. I have won my advantage from that more than once. I once proved a very notorious crime by the crude expedient of impersonating the criminal's victim—a murdered woman—and appearing to him at night before a concealed witness. But spirits are doomed. The present extraordinary wave of superstition and the immense prosperity of the dealers in the 'occult' is a direct result of the war. They are profiteers—every one of them—crystal gazers, mediums, fortune tellers, and the rest. They are reaping a rare harvest for the moment. We punish the humbler rogues, but we don't punish the fools who go to see them. If I had my way, the man or woman who visited the modern witch or wizard should get six months in the second division. Fools should be punished oftener for their folly. But education will sweep these things into the limbo of man's ignorance and mental infancy. Ghosts cannot stand the light of knowledge any better than they can operate in the light of day."

"You are very positive, Mr. Hardcastle."

"Not often—on this subject—yes, Sir Walter Lennox. I have seen too much of the practitioners. Metaphysics is largely to blame. Physics, the strong, you will find far too merciful to metaphysics, the weak."

Sir Walter found himself regarding Hardcastle with dislike. He spoke quietly, yet there was something mocking and annoying in his dogmatism.

"You must discuss the subject with Mr. May, who breakfasted with us. He will, I think, have no difficulty in maintaining the contrary opinion."

"They never have any difficulty—clergymen I mean—and argument with them is vain, because we cannot find common ground to start from. What is the reverend gentleman's theory?"

"He believes that the room holds an invisible and conscious presence permitted to exercise powers of a physical character antagonistic to human life. He is guarded, you see, and will not go so far as to say whether this being is working for good or evil."

"But it has done evil, surely?"

"Evil from our standpoint. But since the Supreme Creator made this creature as well as He made us, therefore Mr. May holds that we are not justified in declaring its operations are evil—save from a human standpoint."

"How was he related to Captain Thomas May?"

"His father."

Peter Hardcastle remained silent for a moment; then he spoke again.

"Have you observed how many of the sons of the clergy go into the Navy or Merchant Marine?"

"I have not."

"They do, however."

Sir Walter began to dislike the detective more than before.

"We will leave you now," he said. "You will find me in my study if you want me. That bell communicates with the servants. The lock of the door was broken when we forced our way in, and has not been mended; but you can close the door if you wish to do so. It has been kept open since and the electric light always turned on at night."

"Many thanks. I will consider a point or two here and rejoin you. Was the chimney examined?"

"No. It would not admit a human being."

Then Sir Walter and his nephew left the room, and Hardcastle, waiting until they were out of earshot, shut the door and thrust a heavy chair against it.

They heard no more of him for an hour, and joined Mary and Septimus May, who were walking on the terrace together. The former was eager to learn the detective's opinions, but her husband's father had already warned her that Peter Hardcastle was doomed to fail.

The four walked up and down together, and Prince, Sir Walter's ancient spaniel, went beside them.

Henry told his cousin the nature of their conversation and the direction in which the professional inquiry seemed to turn.

"He wants to see you and hear everything you can tell him about dear Tom's past," he said.

"Of course I will tell him everything; and what I do not know, Mr. May will remember."

"He is very quiet and very open-minded about some things, but jolly positive about others. Your father-in-law won't get far with him. He scoffs at any supernatural explanation of our terrible loss."

Mr. May overheard this remark.

"As I have already told Mary, his failure is assured. He is wasting his time, and I knew he probably would do so before he came. Not to such a man, however clever he may be, will an explanation be vouchsafed. I would rather trust an innocent child to discover these things than such a person. He is lost in his own conceit and harbors vain ideas."

"There is something about him I cordially dislike already," confessed Sir Walter. "And yet it is a most unreasonable dislike on my part, for he is exceedingly well mannered, speaks and conducts himself like a gentleman, and does nothing that can offend the most sensitive."

"A prejudice, Uncle Walter."

"Perhaps it is, Henry; yet I rarely feel prejudice."

"Call it rather an intuition," said the clergyman. "What your antipathetic attitude means is that you already unconsciously know this man is not going to avail, and that his assumption of superiority in the matter of knowledge—his opinions and lack of faith—will defeat him if nothing else does. He approaches his problem in an infidel spirit, and consequently the problem will evade his skill; because such skill is not merely futile in this matter, but actually destructive."

Mary left them, and they discussed the probable chances of the detective without convincing each other. Henry, who had been much impressed by Hardcastle, argued in his favor; but Septimus May was obdurate, and Sir Walter evidently inclined to agree with him.

"The young men think the old men fools, and the old men know the young ones are," said Sir Walter.

"But he is not young, uncle; he's forty. He told me so."

"I thought him ten years less, and he spoke with the dogmatism of youth."

"Only on that subject."

"Which happens to be the one subject of all others on which we have a right to demand an open and reverent mind," said the clergyman.

Henry noticed that Sir Walter spoke almost spitefully.

"Well, at any rate, he thought rather small beer of the Grey Room. He felt quite sure that the secret lay outside it. He was going to exhaust the possibilities of the place in no time."

As he spoke the gong sounded, and Prince, pricking his ears, led the way to the open French window of the dining-room.

"Call our friend, Henry," said his uncle. And young Lennox, glad of the opportunity, entered the house. He desired a word with Hardcastle in private, and ascended to join him.

The door of the Grey Room was still closed, and Henry found some obstacle within that prevented it from yielding to his hand. At once disturbed by this incident, he did not stand upon ceremony. He pushed the door, which gave before him, and he perceived that a heavy chair had been thrust against it. His noisy entrance challenged no response, and, looking round, it appeared for an instant that the room was empty; but, lowering his eyes, he saw first the detective's open notebook and stylograph lying upon the ground, then he discovered Peter Hardcastle himself upon his face with his arms stretched out before him. He lay beside the hearth, motionless.

Lennox stooped, supported, and turned him over. He was still warm and relaxed in every limb, but quite unconscious and apparently dead. An expression of surprise marked his face, and the corner of each open eye had not yet lost its lustre, but the pupil was much dilated.

CHAPTER VI.

THE ORDER FROM LONDON

Henry Lennox suffered as he had not suffered even during the horrors of war. For the first time in his life he felt fear. He lowered the unconscious man to the ground, and knew that he was dead, for he had looked on sudden death too often to feel in any doubt. Others, however, were not so ready to credit this, and after he hastened downstairs with his evil message, both Sir Walter and Masters found it hard to believe him.

When he descended, his uncle and May were standing at the dining room door, waiting for him and Peter Hardcastle. Mary had just joined them.

"He's dead!" was all the youth could say; then, thoroughly unnerved, he fell into a chair and buried his face in his hands.

Again through his agency had a dead man been discovered in the Grey Room. In each case his had been the eyes first to confront a tragedy, and his the voice to report it. The fact persisted in his mind with a dark obstinacy, as though some great personal tribulation had befallen him.

Mary stopped with her cousin and asked terrified questions, while Sir Walter, calling to Masters, hastened upstairs, followed by Septimus May. The clergyman was also agitated, yet in his concern there persisted a note almost of triumph.

"It is there!" he cried. "It is close to us, watching us, powerless to touch either you or me. But this unhappy sceptic proved an easy victim."

"Would to God I had listened to you yesterday," said Sir Walter. "Then this innocent man had not perhaps been snatched from life."

"You were directed not to listen. Your heart was hardened. His hour had come."

"I cannot believe it. We may restore him. It is impossible that he can be dead in a moment."

They stood over the detective, and Masters and Fred Caunter, with courage and presence of mind, carried him out into the corridor.

The butler spoke.

"Run for the brandy, Fred," he said. "We must get some down his neck if we can. I don't feel the gentleman's heart, but it may not have stopped. He's warm enough."

The footman obeyed, and Hardcastle was laid upon his back. Then Sir Walter directed Masters.

"Hold his head up. It may be better for him."

They waited, and, during the few moments before Caunter returned, Sir Walter spoke again. His mind wandered backward and seemed for the moment incapable of grasping the fact before him.

"Almost the last thing the man said was to ask me why ghosts haunted the night rather than the day."

"Poor fool—poor fool! He is answered," replied the priest.

All attempts to restore the vanished life proved useless, and they carried Hardcastle downstairs presently. Henry Lennox was already gone for the doctor, and when, within an hour, Mannering joined them, he could only pronounce that the man was dead. No sign of life rewarded their protracted efforts to restore circulation. How he had come by his end, how death had broken into his frame, it was impossible to determine. Not an unusual sign marked the body. It revealed neither wound nor outward evidence of shock. The case seemed parallel with that of Thomas May. Death had struck the man like a flash of lightning and dropped him, where he stood, making his notes by the fireplace.

Whereupon a complication faced Dr. Mannering. Mary came to him, where he spoke in the library with Sir Walter and Henry Lennox. She implored him to use his influence with her father-in-law; for they had forgotten Septimus May, while hastily deliberating as to what telegrams should be dispatched; but now they learned that Mr. May was in the Grey Room and refused to leave it.

"He is very excited," she said. "He is walking up and down, speaking aloud, quoting texts from Scripture, addressing the spirit that he believes to be listening to him. It would be grotesque were it not so horrible. He must be made to come away."

"He is justified of his faith," declared Sir Walter. "I have withstood him until now, but I can do so no longer."

"Indeed you must. He is playing with death," said Mannering.

They sought Tom's father, to find him, as Mary had said, walking up and down, with fierce joy of battle on his thin, stern face and in his shining eyes.

"Now shall the powers of Light triumph and the will of God be done!" he said to them.

He made no demur, however, when they drew him away.

"The future is mine," he declared, and grew calm. "You cannot stand between me and my duty again, Sir Walter. You have gravely erred, and this is the result of your error. But you will not err a second time."

His excitation ceased, and it was he who proposed that they should return to their forgotten meal. In the matter of the man just dead, he revealed an indifference almost callous.

"His God will justly judge him according to his deserving," he declared. "If he sinned through ignorance and false teaching, his punishment will not be heavy; if he hardened his heart against truth and rejected the faith from pride—but even then the Father of Mercy may pardon him. He has failed, even as I knew he must, and paid a terrible penalty for failure."

Sir Walter, sorely stricken, hardly heard the other. He ate a little at Mary's entreaty, then, driven by some impulse to leave his fellow-creatures and court solitude, excused himself, begged Lennox and Mannering to bring him news when the telegram dispatched to Scotland Yard was answered, and prepared to leave them.

As he rose, he marked his old spaniel standing whimpering by his side.

"What is the matter with Prince?" he asked.

"He has not had his dinner," said Mary.

"Let him be fed at once," answered her father, and went out alone.

She rose to follow him immediately, but Mannering, who had stopped and was with them, begged her not to do so.

"Leave him to himself," he said. "This has shaken your father, as well it may. He's all right. Make him take his bromide to-night, and let nobody do anything to worry him."

The master of Chadlands meantime went afield, walked half a mile to a favorite spot, and sat down upon a seat that he had there erected. A storm was blowing up from the south-west, and the weather of his mind welcomed it. He alternated between bewilderment and indignation. His own life-long philosophy and trust in the ordered foundations of human existence threatened to fail him entirely before this second stroke. It seemed that the punctual universe was suddenly turned upside down, and had emptied a vial of horror upon his innocent head.

Reality was a thing of the past. A nightmare had taken its place, a nightmare from which there was no waking. He considered the stability of his days—a lifetime followed upon high principles and founded on religious convictions that had comforted his sorrows and countenanced his joys. It seemed a trial undeserved, that in his old age he should be thrust upon a pinnacle of publicity, forced into the public eye, robbed of dignity, denied the privacy he esteemed as the most precious privilege that wealth could command. Stability was destroyed; to count upon the morrow seemed impossible. His thought, strung to a new morbidity, unknown till now, ran on and pictured, with painful, vivid stroke upon stroke, the insufferable series of events that lay before him.

Life was become a bizarre and brutal business for a man of fine feeling. He would be thrust into the pitiless mouth of sensation-mongers, called to appear before tribunals, subjected to an inquisition of his fellow-men, made to endure a notoriety infinitely odious even in anticipation. Indeed, Sir Walter's simple intellect wallowed in anticipation, and so suffered much that, given exercise of restraint, he might have escaped altogether. He was brave enough, but personal bravery would not be called for. He sat now staring dumbly at an imaginary series of events abominable and unseemly in every particular to his order of mind. He was so concerned with what the future must hold in store for him that for a time the present quite escaped his thoughts.

He returned to it, however, and it was almost with the shock of a new surprise he remembered that Peter Hardcastle, a man of European repute, had just died in his house. But he could not in the least realize the new tragedy. He had as yet barely grasped the truth of his son-in-law's end, and still often found himself expecting Tom's footfall and his jolly voice. That such an abundant vitality was stilled, that such an infectious laugh would never sound again on mortal ear he yet sometimes found it hard to believe.

But now it seemed that the impact of this second blow rammed home the first. He brooded upon his dead son-in-law, and it was long before he returned to the event of that day. A thought struck him, and though elementary enough, it seemed to Sir Walter an important conclusion. There could be no shadow of doubt that Tom May and Peter Hardcastle had died by the same secret force. He felt that he must remember this.

Again he puzzled, and then decided with himself that, if he meant to keep sane, he must practice faith and trust in God. Septimus May had said that such unparalleled things some-times happened in the world to try man's faith. Doubtless he was right.

Henceforth the old man determined to stand firmly on the side of the supernatural with the priest. He went further, and blamed his scepticism. It had cost the world a valuable life. He could not, indeed, be censured for that in any court of inquiry. Sceptical men would doubtless say that he had done rightly in refusing Mr. May his experiment. But Sir Walter now convinced himself that he had done wrongly. At such a time, with land-marks vanishing and all accepted laws of matter resolved into chaos, there remained only God to trust. Such a burden as this was not to be borne by any mortal, and Sir Walter determined that he would not bear it.

Were we not told to cast our tribulations before the Almighty? Here, if ever, was a situation beyond the power of human mind to approach, unless a man walked humbly with his hand in his Maker's. Septimus May had been emphatically right. Sir Walter repeated this conviction to himself again and again, like a child.

He descended to details presently. The hidden being, that it had been implicitly agreed could only operate by night in the Grey Room, proved equally potent under noonday sun. But why should it be otherwise? To limit its activities was to limit its powers, and the Almighty alone knew what powers had been granted to it. He shrank from further inquiries or investigations on any but a religious basis. He was now convinced that no natural explanation would exist for what had happened in the Grey Room, and he believed that only through the paths of Christian faith would peace return to him or his house.

Then the present dropped out of his thoughts. They wandered into the past, and he concerned himself with his wife. She it was who had taught him to care for foreign travel. Until his marriage he had hardly left England, save when yachting with friends, and an occasional glimpse of a Mediterranean port was all that Sir Walter knew of the earth outside his own country. But he remembered with gratitude the opportunities won from her. He had taken her round the world, and found himself much the richer in great memories for that experience.

He was still thinking when Mary found him, with his old dog asleep at his feet. She brought him a coat and umbrella, for the threatened storm advanced swiftly under clouds laden with rain. Reluctantly enough he returned to the present. A telegram had been received from London, directing Dr. Mannering to reach the nearest telephone and communicate direct. The doctor was gone to Newton Abbot, and nothing could be done until he came back. Not knowing what had occupied Sir Walter's mind, Mary urged him to leave Chadlands without delay.

"Put the place into the hands of the police and take me with you," she said. "Nothing can be gained by our stopping, and, after this, it is certain the authorities will not rest until they have made a far more searching examination than has ever yet been carried out. They will feel this disaster a challenge."

"Thankfully I would go," he answered. "Most thankfully I would avoid what is hanging over my head. It was terrible enough when your dear husband died; but now we shall be the centre of interest to half England. Every instinct cries to me to get out of it, but obviously that is impossible, even were I permitted to do so. It is the duty of the police to suspect every man and woman under my roof—myself with the rest. These appalling things have occurred in my home, and I must bear the brunt of them and stand up to all that they mean. No Lennox ever ran from his duty, however painful it might be. The death of this man—so eminent in his calling—will attract tremendous attention and be, as you say, a sort of direct challenge to the authorities for whom he worked. They will resent this second tragedy, and with good reason. The poor man, though I cannot pretend that I admired him, was a force for good in the world, and his peculiar genius was devoted to the detection of crime and punishment of criminals—a very worthy occupation, however painful to our ideas."

They sat in the library now, and Henry Lennox spoke to his uncle, with his eye on the window, waiting for the sight of the doctor's car.

"They'll want to tear the place down, very likely. They'll certainly have no mercy on the stones and mortar, any more than they will on us."

"They can spare themselves that trouble, and you your fears," declared Septimus May, who had joined them. "It is impossible that they will be here until to-morrow. Meantime—"

"It is easy to see what they will do," proceeded young Lennox, "and what they will think also. Nor can we prevent them, even if we wanted to. I image their theory will be this. They will suppose that Mr. Hardcastle, left in that room alone, was actually on the track of those responsible for Tom's death. They will guess that, in some way, or by some accident, he surprised the author of the tragedy, and the assassin, seeing his danger, resorted to the same unknown means of murder as before. They may imagine some hidden lunatic concealed here, whose presence is only known to some of us. They may suspect a homicidal maniac in me, or my uncle, or Masters, or anybody. Certainly they will seek a natural explanation and flout the idea of any other."

The clergyman protested, but Henry was not prepared to traverse the old ground again.

"I have as much right to my opinions as you to yours," he said. "And I am positive this is man's work."

Then Mary announced that Mannering's car was in sight. The library windows opened on the western side of the house and afforded a view of the main drive, along which the doctor's little hooded car came flying, like a dead leaf in a storm. But it was not alone. A hospital motor ambulance followed behind it.

They soon learned of curious things, and the house was first thrown into a great bustle and then restored to peace.

Mannering had spoken for half an hour with London, and received directions that puzzled him not a little by their implication. For a moment he seemed unwilling to speak before Mary. Then he begged her bluntly to leave them for a while.

"It's this way," he said when she was gone. "They're harboring a mad idea in London, though, of course, the facts will presently convince them to the contrary. Surely I must know death when

I see it? But a divisional surgeon, or some other medical official, directs me to bring this poor fellow's body to London to-night. Every care must be taken, warmth and air applied, and so on. They've evidently got a notion that, since life appears to go so easily in the Grey Room, and leave no scratch or wound, either life has not gone at all, or that it may be within the power of science to bring it back again. In a sense this is a reflection upon me—as though it were possible that I could make any mistake between death and suspended animation; but I must do as I'm ordered. I travel to town with the dead man to-night, and if they find he is anything but dead as a doornail, I'll—"

The doctor was writing his reminiscences, "The Recollections of a Country Physician," and he could not fail to welcome these events, for they were destined to lend extraordinary attraction to a volume otherwise not destined to be much out of the common.

He spoke again.

"I should be very glad if you would accompany me, Lennox. I shall have a police inspector from Plymouth; but it would be a satisfaction if you could come. Moreover, you would help me in London."

"I'll come up, certainly. You don't mind, Uncle Walter?"

"Not if Mannering wishes it. We owe him more than we can ever repay. Anything that we can do to lessen his labors ought to be done."

"I should certainly welcome your company. A small saloon carriage is to be put on to the Plymouth train that leaves Newton for London before midnight. We shall be met at Paddington by some of their doctors. And as to Chadlands, four men arrive to-morrow morning by the same train that Peter Hardcastle came down in last night. We shall pass them on the way. They will take charge both of the Grey Room and the house as soon as they arrive."

"And they will be welcome. I would myself willingly pull down Chadlands to the foundations if by so doing I could discover the truth."

"It demands no such sacrifice," declared May, who had listened to these facts. "Bricks and mortar, stone and timber are innocent things. One might as soon dissect a thunder-cloud to find the lightning as destroy material substances to discover what is hidden in this house. The unknown being, about his Master's business here, will no more yield its secret to four detectives, or an army of them, than it did to one. 'What I do thou knowest not now.' It is all summed up in that."

He turned to Mannering and asked a sudden question.

"Why did you object to Mary hearing these facts? In what way should they distress her particularly?"

"Can you not see? Indeed, one might fairly have objected to your presence also. But you are a man. There is an implied horror of the darkest sort for poor Mary in the suggestion that Hardcastle may still live. If he can be brought back to life, then she would surely think that perhaps her husband and your son might have been. Imagine the agony of that. I speak plainly; indeed, there is no rational or sentimental reason why I should not, for the truth is, of course, that the signs of death were clearly evident on your poor boy before what we had to do was done. But the bare thought must have shocked Mary. We know emphatically that Hardcastle is dead, and we need not mention to her this fantastic theory from London."

"I appreciate your consideration," said Sir Walter; and the clergyman also acknowledged it.

"There can be no shadow of doubt concerning my son," he said; "nor is there any in the matter of this unfortunate man."

Henry Lennox went to prepare for the journey. Then, obeying the doctor's directions and treating the dead man as though he were merely unconscious, they carried him to the ambulance car. It was an unseemly farce in Mannering's opinion, and he only realized the painful nature of his task when he came to undertake it; but he carried it through in every particular as directed, conveyed the corpse to Newton after dark, and had the ambulance bed, in which it reposed, borne to the saloon carriage when the night mail arrived from Plymouth, between eleven and twelve. He was able to regulate the temperature with hot steam, and kept hot bottles to the feet and sides of the dead.

He felt impatient and resentful; he poured scorn on the superior authority for the benefit of the inspector and Henry Lennox, who accompanied him; but in secret he experienced emotions of undoubted satisfaction that life had broken from its customary monotonous round to furnish him with an adventure so unique. He pointed out a fact to the policeman before they had started.

"You will observe," he said, with satire, "that, despite the heat we are directed to apply to this unfortunate man, rigor mortis has set in. Whether the authority in London regards that as an evidence of death, of course I cannot pretend to say. Perhaps not. I may be behind the times."

Neither Mannering nor Lennox had spared much thought for those left behind them at Chadlands. The extraordinary character of the task put upon them sufficed to fill their minds, and it was not until the small hours, when they sat with their hands in their pockets and the train ran steadily through darkness and storm, that the younger spoke of his cousin.

"I hope those old men won't bully Mary to-night," he said. "I'd meant to ask you to give Uncle Walter a caution. May's not quite all there, in my opinion, and very likely, now you're out of the way, he'll get round Sir Walter about that infernal room."

Mannering became interested.

"D'you mean for an instant he wants to try his luck after what's happened?"

"You forget. Your day has been so full that you forget what did happen."

"I do not, Lennox. Mary begged me to tackle the man. I calmed him, and he came down to his luncheon. He must have thought over the matter since then, and seen that he was playing with death."

"Far from it, 'The future is mine!' That's what he said. And that means he'll try and be in the Grey Room alone to-night."

"I wish to Heaven you'd made this clear before we'd started. But surely we can trust Sir Walter; he knows what this means, even if that superstitious lunatic doesn't."

"I don't want to bother you," answered Henry; "but, looking back, I'm none so sure that we can trust my uncle. He's been pretty wild to-day, and who shall blame him? Things like this crashing into his life leave him guessing. He's very shaken, and has lost his mental grip, too. Reality's played him such ugly tricks that he may be tempted to fall back on unreality now."

"You don't mean he'll let May go into that room to-night?"

"I hope not. He was firm enough last night when the clergyman clamored to do so. In fact, he made me keep watch to see he didn't. But I think he's weakened a lot since Hardcastle came to grief in broad daylight. And I sha'n't be there to do anything."

"All this comes too late," answered the other. "If harm has happened—it has happened. We can only pray they've preserved some sanity among them."

"That's why I say I hope they're not bullying Mary," answered Lennox. "Of course, she'd be dead against her father-in-law's idea. But she won't count. She can't control him if Sir Walter goes over to his side."

"Let us not imagine anything so unreasonable. We'll telegraph to hear if all's well at the first moment we can."

The storm sent a heavy wash of rain against the side of the carriage. It was a famous tempest, that punished the South of England from Land's End to the North Foreland.

They were distracted from their thoughts by the terrific impact of the wind.

"Wonder we can stop on the rails," said Mannering. "This is a fifty-knot gale, or I'm mistaken."

"I'm thinking of the Chadlands trees," answered the other. "It's rum how, in the middle of such an awful business as this, the mind switches off to trifles. Does it on purpose, I suppose, to relieve the strain. Yes, the trees will catch it to-night. I expect I shall hear a grim tale of fallen timber from Sir Walter by the time I get back to-morrow."

"If nothing's fallen but timber, I sha'n't mind," answered Mannering; "but you've made me devilish uneasy now. If anything further went wrong—well, to put it mildly, they would say your uncle ought to have known a great deal better."

"He does know a great deal better. It's only that temporarily he's knocked off his balance. But I hardly feel as anxious as you do. There's Mary against May; and even if my uncle were for him, on a general, vague theory of something esoteric and outside nature, which you can't fairly call unreasonable any more, Mannering, seeing what's happened—even if Sir Walter felt tempted to let him have his way, I don't believe he'd really consent when it came to the point."

"I hope not—I hope not," answered the other. "Such a concession would take a lot of explanation if the result were another of these disasters. There ought to be an official guard over the room."

"After to-morrow there certainly will be," replied Henry. "You may be sure the police won't leave it again till they've satisfied themselves. All the same, I don't see how a dozen of them will be any safer than one—even if it's some material and physical thing that happens, as we must suppose. And for that matter, if it's really supernatural, why should a dozen be safer than one? Obviously they wouldn't. Whatever it is, it can strike as it likes and without being struck back."

But Dr. Mannering did not answer these questions. He was considering a little book in his pocket, which he would hand over to the police in London next morning.

"Poor chap—if he could have begun by taking the problem by the throat, as he has written here. But, instead, it took him by the throat!"

He took Hardcastle's notebook from his pocket and read again the last few pages.

"He was dreaming of his theories to the last, when he should surely have been girt up in every limb to face facts," said Lennox. "He never realized the horrible danger."

Perusal of the detective's data had revealed an interesting fact. It was known by his colleagues that he designed a book on the theory and practice of criminal investigations, and in many of his pocket-books, subsequently examined, were found memoranda and jottings, doubtless destined to be worked out at another time. It was clear that he had, for a few moments, drifted away from the Grey Room in thought when his death overtook him. Past events, not present problems, were apparently responsible for the reflections that occupied his mind. He was not concentrating on the material phenomena actually under his observation when he died, but following some private meditations provoked by his experiences.

"Elimination embraces the secret of success," he had written. "Exercise the full force of your intelligence and spare no pains to eliminate from every case all matter not bearing directly upon the actual problem. Nine times out of ten the issue is direct, and once permit side issues to draw their tracks across it, once admit metaphysical lines of reasoning, the result will be confusion and a problem increasing in complexity at every stage. Only in romances, where a plot is invented and then complicated by deliberate art, shall we find the truth ultimately permitted to appear in some subordinate incident, or individual, studiously kept in the background—that is the craft of telling detective stories. But, in truth, one needs to lay hold of the problem by the throat at the outset. Deception is too much the province of the criminal and too little the business of the investigator; and where it may be possible to creep, like a snake, into a case, unknown for what you truly are, then your opportunities and chances of success are enormously increased. It is, however, the exception when one can start without the knowledge of anybody involved, and the Scotland Yard of the future will pursue its business under very different circumstances from the present. The detective's work should be made easier and not more difficult. None should know who is working on a case. The law's representatives should be disguised and move among the characters surrounding the crime as something other than they really are. They will—"

Here Hardcastle's reflections came to an end. Some previous notes there were of superficial accidents in the Grey Room and a rough ground plan of it; but nothing more. He had evidently, for the time being, broken away from his environment and was merely thinking, with a pen on paper, when he died.

CHAPTER VII.

THE FANATIC

A succession of incidents, that must have perturbed the doctor and his companion in earnest, had followed upon their departure from Chadlands, and Mary soon discovered that she was faced with a terrible problem.

For one young woman had little chance of winning her way against an old man and the religious convictions that another had impressed upon him. Sir Walter and the priest were now at one, nor did the common sense of a fourth party to the argument convince them. At dinner Septimus May declared his purpose.

"We are happily free of any antagonistic and material influence," he said. "Providence has willed that those opposed to us should be taken elsewhere, and I am now able to do my duty without more opposition."

"Surely, father, you do not wish this?" asked Mary. "I thought you—"

But the elder was fretful.

"Let me eat my meal in peace," he answered. "I am not made of iron, and reason cuts both ways. It was reasonable to deny Mr. May before these events. It would be unreasonable to pretend that the death of Peter Hardcastle has not changed my opinions. To cleave to the possibility of a physical explanation any longer is mere folly and obstinacy. I believe him to be right."

"This is fearful for me—and fearful for everybody here. Don't you see what it would mean if anything happened to you, Mr. May? Even supposing there is a spirit hidden in the Grey Room with power and permission to destroy us—why, that being so, are you any safer than dear Tom was or this poor man?"

"Because I am armed, Mary, and they were defenseless. Unhappily youth is seldom clothed in the whole armor of righteousness. My dear son was a good and honorable man, but he was not a religious man. He had yet to learn the incomparable and vital value of the practice of Christian faith. Hardcastle invited his own doom. He admitted—he even appeared to pride himself upon a crude and pagan rationalism. It is not surprising that such a man should be called away to learn the lessons of which he stood so gravely in need."

"I know that our dear Tom was bidden to higher work—to labor in a higher cause than here, to purer knowledge of those things that matter most to the human soul," said Mary. "But that is not to say God chose to take him by a miracle. For what you believe amounts to a miracle. You know that I am bearing my loss in the same spirit as yourself, but, granted it had to be at God's will, that is no reason why we should suppose the means employed were outside nature."

"How can you pretend they are inside nature, as we know it?" asked her father.

"We know nothing at all yet, and I implore Mr. May to wait until we are at least assured that science cannot find a reason."

"Fear not for me, my child," answered Septimus May. "You forget certain details that have assisted to decide me. Remember that Hardcastle had openly denied and derided the possibility of supernatural peril. He had challenged this potent thing not an hour before he was brought face to face with it. Tom went to his death innocently; this man cannot be absolved so easily. In my case, with my knowledge and faith, the conditions are very different, and I oppose an impregnable barrier between myself and the secret being. I am an old priest, and I go knowing the nature of my task. My weapons are such that a good spirit would applaud them and an evil spirit be powerless against them. Do you not see that the Almighty could never permit one of His creatures—for even the devils also are His—to defeat His own minister or trample on the name of Christ? It would amount to that. So armed one might walk in safety through the lowermost hell, for hell can only believe and tremble before the truth."

Mary looked hopelessly at her father; but he offered her small comfort. Sir Walter still found himself conforming to the fierce piety and dogmatic assurance of the man of God. In this welter and upheaval his modest intellect found only a foothold here, and his judgment now firmly inclined to the confident assertions of religion. He was himself a devout and conventional believer, and he turned to the support of faith, and shared, with increasing conviction, the opinion of Septimus May, as uttered in a volume of confident words. He became blind to the physical danger. He even showed a measure of annoyance at Mary's obstinate entreaties. She strove to calm him, and told him he was not himself—an assertion that, by his inner consciousness of its truth, seemed to incense Sir Walter.

He begged her to be silent, and declared that her remarks savored of irreverence. Startled and bewildered by such a criticism, the woman was indeed silent for some time, while her father-in-law flowed on and uttered his conviction. Yet not all his intensity and asseverations could justify such extravagant assertion. At another time they might even have amused Mary; but in sight of the fact that her father was yielding, and that the end of the argument would mean the clergyman in the Grey Room, she could win nothing but frantic anxiety from the situation. Sir Walter was broken; he had lost his hold on reality, and she realized that. His unsettled intelligence had gone over to the opposition, and there was none, as it seemed, to argue on her side.

Septimus May had acted like a dangerous drug on Sir Walter; he appeared to be intoxicated in some degree. But only in mind, not in manner. He argued for his new attitude, and he was not as excited as the priest, but maintained his usual level tones.

"I agreed with Mannering and Henry yesterday, as you know, Mary," he said, "and at my desire Mr. May desisted from his wish. We see how mistaken I was, how right he must have been. I have thought it out this afternoon, calmly and logically. These unfortunate young men have died without a reason, for be sure no explanation of Peter Hardcastle's death will be forthcoming though the whole College of Surgeons examines his corpse. Then we must admit that life has been snatched out of these bodies by some force of which we have no conception. Were it natural, science would have discovered a reason for death; but it could not, because their lives flowed away as water out of a bottle, leaving the bottle unchanged in every particular. But life does not desert its physical habitation on these terms. It cannot quit a healthy, human body neither ruined nor rent. You must be honest with yourself, my child, as well as with your father-in-law and me. A physical cause being absolutely ruled out, what remains? To-night I emphatically support Mr. May, and my conscience, long in terrible concern, is now at rest again.

And because it is at rest, I know that I have done well. I believe that what dear Tom's father desires to do—namely, to spend this night in the Grey Room—is now within his province and entirely proper to his profession, and I share his perfect faith and confidence."

"It is you who lack faith, Mary," continued Septimus May. "You lack faith, otherwise you would appreciate the unquestionable truth of what your father tells you. Listen," he continued, "and understand something of what this means from a larger outlook than our own selfish and immediate interests. Much may come of my action for the Faith at large. I may find an answer to those grave questions concerning the life beyond and the whole problem of spiritualism now convulsing the Church and casting us into opposing sections. It is untrodden and mysterious ground; but I am called upon to tread it. For my part, I am never prepared to flout inquirers if they approach these subjects in a reverent spirit. We must not revile good men because they think differently from ourselves. We must examine the assertions of such inquirers as Sir Oliver Lodge and Sir Conan Doyle in a mood of reverence and sympathy. Some men drift away from the truth in vital particulars; but not so far that they cannot return if the road is made clear to them.

"We must remember that our conviction of a double existence rests on the revelation of God through His Son, not on a mere, vague desire toward a future life common to all sorts and conditions of men. They suspected and hoped; we know. Science may explain that general desire if it pleases; it cannot explain, or destroy, the triumphant certainty born of faith. Spiritualism has succeeded to the biblical record of 'possession,' and I, for my part, of course prefer what my Bible teaches. I do not myself find that the 'mediums' of modern spiritualism speak with tongues worthy of much respect up to the present, and it is certain that rogues abound; but the question is clamant. It demands to be discussed by our spiritual guides and the fathers of the Church. Already they recognize this fact and are beginning to approach it—some priests in a right spirit, some—as at the Church Congress last month—in a wrong spirit."

"A wrong spirit, May?" asked Sir Walter.

"In my opinion, a wrong spirit," answered the other. "There is much, even in a meeting of the Church Congress, that makes truly religious men mourn. They laughed when they should have learned. I refer to incidents and criticisms of last October. There the Dean of Manchester, who shows how those, who have apparently spoken to us from Beyond through the mouths of living persons, describe their different states and conditions. Stainton Moses gave us a vision of heaven such as an Oxford don and myself might be supposed to appreciate.

"Raymond describes a heaven wherein the average second lieutenant could find all that, for the moment, he needs. But why laugh at these things? If we make our own hells, shall we not make our own heavens? We must go into the next world more or less cloyed and clogged with the emotions and interests of this one. It is inevitable. We cannot instantly throw off a lifetime of interests, affections, and desires. We are still human and pass onward as human beings, not as angels of light.

"Therefore, we may reasonably suppose that the Almighty will temper the wind to the shorn lamb, nor impose too harsh and terrible a transformation upon the souls of the righteous departed, but lead one and all, by gradual stages and through not unfamiliar conditions, to the heaven of ultimate and absolute perfection that He has designed for His conscious creatures."

"Well spoken," said Sir Walter.

But Mr. May had not finished. He proceeded to the immediate point.

"Shall it be denied that devils have been cast out in the name of God?" he asked. "And if from human tenements, then why not from dwellings made with human hands also? May not a house be similarly cleansed as well as a soul? This unknown spirit—angel or fiend, or other sentient being—is permitted to challenge mankind and draw attention to its existence. A mystery, I grant, but its Maker has now willed that some measure of this mystery shall be revealed to us. We are called to play our part in this spirit's existence.

"It would seem that it has endured a sort of imprisonment in this particular room for more years than we know, and it may actually be the spirit of some departed human being condemned, for causes that humanity has forgotten, to remain within these walls. The nameless and unknown thing cries passionately to be liberated, and is permitted by its Maker to draw our terrified attention upon itself by the exercise of destructive functions transcending our reason.

"God, then, has willed that, through the agency of devout and living men, the unhappy phantom shall now be translated and moved from this environment for ever; and to me the appointed task is allotted. So I believe, as firmly as I believe in the death and resurrection of the Lord. Is that clear to you, Sir Walter?"

"It is. You have made it convincingly clear."

"So be it, then. I, too, Mary, am not dead to the meaning of science in its proper place. We may take an illustration of what I have told you from astronomy. As comets enter our system from realms of which we have no knowledge, dazzle us a little, awaken our speculations and then depart, so may certain immortal spirits also be supposed to act. We entangle them possibly in our gross air and detain them for centuries, or moments, until their Creator's purpose in sending them is accomplished. Then He takes the means to liberate them and set them on their eternal roads and to their eternal tasks once more."

The listening woman, almost against her reason, felt herself beginning to share these assumptions. But that they were fantastic, unsupported by any human knowledge, and would presently involve an experiment full of awful peril to the life of the man who uttered them, she also perceived. Yet her reasonable caution and conventional distrust began to give way a little under the priest's magnetic voice, his flaming eyes, his positive and triumphant certainty of truth. He burned with his inspiration, and she felt herself powerless to oppose any argument founded on facts against the mystic enthusiasm of such religious faith. His honesty and fervor could not, however, abate Mary's acute fear. Her father had entirely gone over to the side of the devotee and she knew it.

"It is well we have your opportunity to-night," he said, "for had the police arrived, out of their ignorance they might deny it to you."

Yet Mary fought on against them. In despair she appealed to Masters. He had been an officer's orderly in his day, and when he left the Army and came to Chadlands, he never departed again. He was an intelligent man, who occupied a good part of his leisure in reading. He set Sir Walter and Mary first in his affections; and that Mary should have won him so completely she always held to be a triumph, since Abraham Masters had no regard or admiration for women.

"Can't you help me, Masters?" she begged. "I'm sure you know as well as I do that this ought not to happen."

The butler eyed his master. He was handing coffee, but none took it.

"By all means speak," said Sir Walter. "You know how I rate your judgment, Masters. You have heard Mr. May upon this terrible subject, and should be convinced, as I am."

Masters was very guarded.

"It's not for me to pass an opinion, Sir Walter. But the reverend gentleman, no doubt, understands such things. Only there's the Witch of Endor, if I may mention the creature, she fetched up more than she bargained for. And I remember a proverb as I heard in India, from a Hindoo. I've forgot the lingo now, but I remember the sense. They Hindoos say that if you knock long enough at a closed door, the devil will open it—excuse my mentioning such a thing; but Hindoos are awful wise."

"And what then, Masters? I know not who may open the door of this mystery; but this I know, that, in the Name of the Most High God, I can face whatever opens it."

"I ain't particular frightened neither, your reverence," said Masters. "But I wouldn't chance it alone, being about average sinful and not near good enough to tackle that unknown horror hid up there single-handed. I'd chance it, though, in high company like yours. And that's something."

"It is, Masters, and much to your credit," declared Sir Walter. "For that matter, I would do the like. Indeed, I am willing to accompany Mr. May."

While Septimus May shook his head and Mary trembled, the butler spoke again.

"But there's nobody else in this house would. Not even Fred Caunter, who doesn't know the meaning of fear, as you can testify, Sir Walter. But he's fed up with the Grey Room, if I may say so, and so's the housekeeper, Mrs. Forbes, and so's Jane Bond. Not that they would desert the ship; but there's others that be going to do so. I may mention that four maids and Jackson intend to give notice to-morrow. Ann Maine, the second housemaid, has gone to-night. Her father fetched her. Excuse me mentioning it, but Mrs. Forbes will give you the particulars to-morrow, if you please."

"Hysteria," declared Sir Walter. "I don't blame them. It is natural. Everybody is free to go, if they desire to do so. But tell them what you have heard to-night, Masters. Tell them that no good Christian need fear to rest in peace. Explain that Mr. May will presently enter the Grey Room in the name of God; and bid them pray on their knees for him before they go to sleep."

Masters hesitated.

"All the same, I very much wish the reverend gentleman would give Scotland Yard a chance. If they fall, then he can wipe their eye after—excuse my language, Sir Walter. I've read a lot about the spirits, being terrible interested in 'em, as all human men must be; and I hear that running after 'em often brings trouble. I don't mean to your life, Sir Walter, but to your wits. People get cracked on 'em and have to be locked up. I stopped everybody frightening themselves into 'sterics at dinner to-day; but you could see how it took 'em; and, whether or no, I do beg Mr. May to be so kind as to let me sit up along with him to-night.

"You never hear of two people getting into trouble with these here customers, and while he was going for this blackguard ghost in the name of the Lord, I could keep my weather eye lifting for trouble. 'Tis a matter for common sense and keeping your nerve, in my opinion, and we don't want another death on our hands, I suppose. There'll be half the mountebanks and photograph men and newspaper men in the land here to-morrow, and 'twill take me all my time to keep 'em from over-running the house. Because if they could come in their scores for the late captain—poor gentleman!—what won't they try now this here famous detective has been done in?"

"Henry deplored the same thing," said Mary. "And I answer again, as I answered then," replied Septimus May. "You mean well, Sir Walter, and your butler means well; but you propose an act in direct opposition to the principle that inspires me."

"What do you expect to happen?" asked Mary. "Do you suppose you will see something, and that something will tell you what it is, and why it killed dear Tom?"

"That, at any rate, would be a very great blessing to the living," said her father.

"The least the creature could do, in my humble opinion," ventured Masters.

But Septimus May deprecated such curiosity.

"Hope for no such thing, and do not dwell upon what is to happen until I am able to tell you what does happen," he answered. "Allow no human weakness, no desire to learn the secrets of another world, to distract your thoughts. I am only concerned with what I know beyond possibility of doubt is my duty—to be entered upon as swiftly as possible. I hear my call in the very voice of the wind shouting round the house to-night. But beyond my duty I do not seek. Whether information awaits me, whether some manifestation indicating my success and valuable to humanity will be granted, I cannot say. I do not stop now to think about that.

"Alone I do this thing—yet not alone, for my hand is in my Maker's hand. Your part will not be to accompany me. Let each man and woman be informed of what I do, and let them lift a petition for me, that my work be crowned with success. But let them not assume that to-morrow I shall have anything to impart. The night may be one of peace within, though so stormy without. I may pray till dawn with no knowledge how my prayer prospers, or I may be called to face a being that no human eye has ever seen and lived. These things are hidden from us."

"You are wonderful, and it is heartening to meet with such mighty faith," replied Sir Walter. "You have no fear, no shadow of hesitation or doubt at the bottom of your mind?"

"None. Only an overmastering desire to obey the message

that throbs in my heart. I will be honest with you, for I recognize that many might doubt whether you were in the right to let me face this ordeal. But I am driven by an overwhelming mandate. Did I fear, or feel one tremor of uncertainty, I would not proceed; for any wavering might be fatal and give me helpless into the power of this watchful spirit; but I am as certain of my duty as I am that salvation awaits the just man.

"I believe that I shall liberate this arrested being with cathartic prayer and cleansing petition to our common Maker. And have I not the spirit of my dead boy on my side? Could any living man, however well intentioned, watch with me and over me as he will? Fear nothing; go to your rest, and let all who would assist me do so on their knees before they sleep."

Even Masters echoed some of this fierce and absolute faith when he returned to the servants' hall.

"His eyes blaze," he said. "He's about the most steadfast man ever I saw inside a pulpit, or out of it. You feel if that man went to the window and told the rain to stop and the wind to go down, they would. No ghost that ever walked could best him anyway. They asked me to talk and say what I felt, and I did; but words are powerless against such an iron will as he's got.

"I doubted first, and Sir Walter said he doubted likewise; but he's dead sure now, and what's good enough for him is good enough for us. I'll bet Caunter, or any man, an even flyer that he's going to put the creature down and out and come off without a scratch himself. I offered to sit up with him, so did Sir Walter; but he wouldn't hear of it. So all we've got to do is to turn in and say our prayers. That's simple enough for God-fearing people, and we can't do no better than to obey orders."

It was none the less a nervous and highly strung household that presently went to bed, and no woman slept without another woman to keep her company. Sir Walter found himself worn out in mind and body. Mary made him take his bromide, and he slept without a dream, despite the din of the great "sou'-wester" and the distant, solemn crash of more than one great tree thrown upon the lap of mother earth at last.

Before he retired, however, something in the nature of a procession had escorted the priest to his ordeal. Mr. May donned biretta, surplice, and stole, for, as he explained, he was to hold a religious service as sacred and significant as any other rite.

"Lord send him no congregation then," thought Masters.

But, with Sir Walter and Mary, he followed the ministrant, and left him at the open door of the Grey Room. The electric light shone steadily; but the storm seemed to beat its fists at the windows, and the leaded panes shook and chattered. With no bell and candle, but his Bible alone, Septimus May entered the room, having first made the sign of the Cross before him; then he turned and bade good-night to all.

"Be of good faith!" were the last words he spoke to them.

Having done so he shut the door, and they heard his voice immediately uplifted in prayer. They waited a little, and the sound rolled steadily on. Sir Walter then bade Masters extinguish all the lights and send the household to bed, though the time was not more than ten o'clock.

As for Masters, the glamour and appeal of those strenuous words at the dinner-table had now passed, and presently, as he prepared to retire, he found himself far less confident and assured than his recent words had implied. He sank slowly from hope to fear, even pictured the worse, and asked himself what would follow if the worst happened. He believed that it might mean serious disaster for Sir Walter. If another life were sacrificed to this unknown peril, and it transpired that his master had sanctioned what would amount to suicide in the eyes of reason; then he began to fear that grave trouble must result. Already the burning words of Septimus May began to cool and sound unreal, and Masters suspected that, if they were repeated in other ears, which had not heard him utter them, or seen the fervor of religious earnestness and reverence in which they had been spoken, this feverish business of exorcising a ghost in the twentieth century might only awake derision and receive neither credence nor respect. His entire concern was for Sir Walter, not Mr. May. He could not sleep, lighted a pipe, considered whether it was in his power to do anything, felt a sudden impulse to take certain steps, yet hesitated—from no fear to himself, but doubt whether action might not endanger another. Mary did not sleep either, and she suffered more, for she had never approved, and now she blamed herself not a little for her weak opposition. A thousand arguments occurred to her while she lay awake. Then, for a time, she forgot present tribulations, and her own grief overwhelmed her, as it was wont to do by night. For while the events that had so swiftly followed each other since her husband's death banished him now and again, save from her subconscious mind, when alone he was swift to return and her sorrow made many a night sleepless. She was herself ill, but did not know it. The reaction had yet to come, and could not be long delayed, for her nervous energy was worn out now. She wept and lived days with the dead; then the present returned to her mind, and she fretted and prayed—for Septimus May and for daylight. She wondered why stormy nights were always the longest. She heard a thousand unfamiliar sounds, and presently leaped from her bed, put on a dressing-gown, and crept out into the house. To know that all was well with the watcher would hearten her. But then her feet dragged before she had left the threshold of her own room, and she stood still and shuddered a little. For how if all were not well? How if his voice no longer sounded?

She hesitated to make the experiment, and balanced the relief of reassurance against the horror of silence. She remembered a storm at sea, when through a long night, not lacking danger to a laboring steamer with weak engines, she had lain awake and felt her heart warm again when the watch shouted the hour.

She set out, then, determined to know if all prospered with her father-in-law. Nor would she give ear to misgiving or ask herself what she would do if no voice were steadily uplifted in the Grey Room.

The great wind seemed to play upon Chadlands like a harp. It roared and reverberated, now stilled a moment for another leap, now died away against the house, yet still sounded with a steady shout in the neighbor trees. At the casements it tugged and rattled; against them it flung the rain fiercely. Every bay and passage of the interior uttered its own voice, and overhead was creaking of old timbers, rattling of old slates, and rustling of mortar fragments dislodged by sudden vibrations.

Mary proceeded on her way, and then, to her astonishment, heard a footfall, and nearly ran into an invisible figure approaching from the direction of the Grey Room. Man and woman startled each other, but neither exclaimed, and Mrs. May spoke.

"Who is it?" she asked; and Masters answered:

"Oh, my gracious! Terrible sorry, ma'am! If I didn't think—"

"What on earth are you doing, Masters?"

"Much the same as you, I expect, ma'am. I thought just to creep along and see if the reverend gentleman was all right. And he is. The light's burning—you can see it under the door—and he's praying away, steady as a steam-threshing machine. I doubt he's keeping the evil creature at arm's length, and I'm a tidy lot more hopeful than what I was an hour ago. The thing ain't strong enough to touch a man praying to God like what he can. But if prayers keep it harmless, then it's got ears and it's alive!"

"Can you believe that, Masters?" she whispered.

"Got to, ma'am. If it was just a natural horror beyond the reach of prayer, it would have knocked his reverence out long before now, like other people. It settled the police officer in under an hour, and Mr. May's been up against it for three—nearly four hours, so far. He'll bolt it yet, I shouldn't wonder, like a ferret bolts a rat."

"You really feel more hopeful?"

"Yes, I do, ma'am; and if he can fire the creature and signal 'All's clear' for Chadlands, it will calm everybody and be a proper feather in his cap, and he did ought to be made a bishop, at the least. Not that Scotland Yard men will believe a word of it to-morrow, all the same. Ghosts are bang out of their line, and I never met even a common constable that believed in 'em, except Bob Parrett, and he had bats in the belfry, poor chap. No; they'll reckon it's somebody in the house, I expect, who wanted to kill t' others, but ain't got no quarrel with Mr. May. And you'd be wise to get back to bed, ma'am, and try to sleep, else you'll catch a cold. I'll look round again in an hour or to, if I don't go to sleep my self."

They parted, while the storm still ran high, and through the empty corridor, when it was lulled, a voice rolled steadily on from the Grey Boom.

When it suddenly ceased, an hour before dawn, the storm had already begun to sink, and through a rack of flying and breaking cloud the "Hunter" wheeled westerly to his setting.

CHAPTER VIII.

THE LABORS OF THE FOUR

Despite the storm, Sir Walter slept through the night, and did not waken until his man drew the blinds upon a dawn sky so clear that it seemed washed of its blue. He had directed to be wakened at six o'clock.

"What of Mr. May?" he asked.

"Masters wants to know if we shall call him, Sir Walter."

"Not if he has returned to his room, but immediately if still in the Grey Room."

"He's not in his own room, sir."

"Then seek him at once."

The valet hesitated.

"Please, Sir Walter, there's none much cares to open the door."

He heard his daughter's voice outside at the same moment.

"Mr. May has not left the Grey Room, father."

"I'll be with you in a moment," he answered.

Then he rose, dressed partially, and joined her. She was full of active fear.

"All went well at two o'clock," she said, "for I crept out to listen. So did Masters. Mr. May's voice sounded clear and steady."

They found the butler at the door of the Grey Room. He was pale and mopping his forehead.

"I've called to him, but it's as silent as the grave in there," he said. "It's all up with the gentleman; I know it!"

"He may not be there; he may have gone out," answered Sir Walter.

Then he opened the door widely and entered. The electric light still shone and killed the pallid white stare of the morning. Upon a little table under it they observed Septimus May's Bible, open at an epistle of St. Paul, but the priest himself was on the floor some little distance away. He lay in a huddled heap of his vestments. He had fallen upon his right side apparently, and, though the surplice and cassock which he had worn were disarranged, he appeared peaceful enough, with his cheek on a foot stool, as though disposed deliberately upon the ground to sleep. His biretta was still upon his head; his eyes were open, and the fret and passion manifested by his face in life had entirely left it. He looked many years younger, and no emotion of any kind marked his placid countenance. But he was dead; his heart had ceased to beat and his extremities were already cold. The room appeared unchanged in every particular. As in the previous cases, death had come by stealth, yet robbed, as far as the living could judge, of all terror for its victim.

Masters called Caunter and Sir Walter's valet, who stood at the door. The latter declined to enter or touch the dead, but Caunter obeyed, and together the two men lifted Mr. May and carried him to his own room. In a moment it seemed that the house knew what had happened.

A scene of panic and hysteria followed below stairs, and, without Jane Bond's description of it, Mary knew the people were running out of the house as from a plague. She left her father with Masters, and strove to calm the frightened domestics. She spoke well, and explained that the event, horrible though it was, yet proved that no cause for their alarm any longer existed.

"If it had been a wicked spirit we do not understand, it would have had no power over Mr. May, who was a saint of God," she said. "Be at peace, restrain yourselves, and fear nothing now. There is no ghost here. Had it been a demon or any such thing, it must have been conscious, and therefore powerless against Mr. May. This proves that there is some fearful natural danger which we have not yet discovered hidden in the room, but no harm can happen to anybody if they do not go into the room. The police are coming from Scotland Yard in an hour or two, and you may feel as sure, as I do, and Sir Walter does, that they will find out the truth, whatever it is. You must none of you think of leaving before they come. If you do, they will only send for you again. Please prepare your breakfast and be reasonable. Sir Walter is terribly upset, and it would be a base thing if any of you were to desert him at a moment like this."

They grew steadier before her, and Mrs. Forbes, the housekeeper, who believed what Mary had said, added her voice.

Then Sir Walter's daughter returned to her father, who was with Masters in the study. A man had already started for a doctor, but with Mannering away there was none nearer than Neon Abbot.

Mary called on Masters to assert his authority, and reassure the household as she had done. She told him her argument, and he accepted it as a revelation.

"Thank God you could keep your senses and see that, ma'am! Tell the master the same, and make him drink a drop of spirits and get into his clothes. He's shook cruel!"

He had already brought the brandy, which was his panacea for all ills, and now left Mary and her father together. She found him collapsed, and forgot the cause for a few moments in her present concern for him. Indeed, she always thought, and often said afterwards, that but for the minor needs for action that intervened in this series of terrible moments she must herself have gone out of her mind. But something always happened, as in this case, to demand her full attention, and so arrest and deflect the strain almost at the moment of its impact.

She found that the ideas she had just employed to pacify the servants' hall were also in her father's thoughts. From them, however, he won no consolation, though he stood convinced. But the fact that Septimus May should have failed, and paid for his failure with his life, now assumed its true significance for Sir Walter. He was self-absorbed, prostrate, and desperate. In such a condition one is not master of oneself, and may say and do anything. The old man's armor was off, and in the course of his next few speeches, by a selfish forgetfulness that he would have been the first to condemn in another, he revealed a thing that was destined to cause the young widow bitter and needless pain. First, however, he pointed out what she already grasped and made clear to others.

"This upsets all May's theories and gives the lie to me as well. Why did I believe him! Why did I let him convince me against my better judgment?"

"Do not fret about that now."

"You might say, 'I told you so!' but you will not do that. Nevertheless, you were right to seek to stop this unfortunate man last night, and he was terribly mistaken. No being from another world had anything to do with his death. If we granted that, there is an end of religious faith."

"We can be sure of it, father. Evil spirits would have had no power over Mr. May, if there is a just God in heaven."

"Then it is something else. If not a spirit, then a living man—a human devil—and the police will discover him. In this house, one we have known and trusted; for all are known and trusted. They will blame me, with good reason, for sacrificing another life. The irony of fate that I, of all men, one so much alive to the meaning of mercy—that I, out of superstitious folly—But how will it look in the eyes of justice? Black—black! I am well prepared to suffer what I have deserved, Mary. Nothing that man can do to me equals the shame and dismay I feel when I consider what I have done to myself!"

"You must not talk so; it is unworthy of you. You know it, father, while you speak. Nobody has a right to question you or your opinions. Many would have been convinced by Mr. May last night. They may still think that he was right, and that, far from receiving evil treatment, he was blessed by being taken away into the next world without pain or shock. We must feel for him as we try to feel for dear Tom. And I do not mean that I am sorry for him; I am only sorry for us, because of the difficulty of explaining. Yet to tell the truth will not be difficult. They must do the best they can. It doesn't matter as much as you think. Indeed, how should they blame you at all until they themselves find out the truth?"

"They will—they must! They will discover the reason. They will hunt down the murderer, and they will inevitably attach utmost blame to me for listening to a man possessed. May was possessed, I tell you!"

"He was exceedingly convincing. When I listened to him he shook me, too."

"I should have supported you, instead of going over to him."

"He knows the truth now. He is with Tom now. We must

remember that. We know they are happy, and that makes the opinion of living people matter very little."

Then, out of his weakness, he smote her, and thrust upon her some hours of agony, very horrible in their nature, which there was no good reason that Mary should have suffered.

"Who is alive and who is dead?" he asked. "We don't even know that. The police demanded to make their own inquiries, and Peter Hardcastle may at this moment be a living and breathing man, if they are right."

She stared at him and feared for his reason.

"What do you mean?"

"I mean that they were not prepared to grant that he was dead. Henry and Mannering took him up on that assumption. He may have been restored to animation and his vital forces recovered. Why not? There was nothing visible to indicate dissolution. We have heard of trances, catalepsies, which simulate death so closely that even physicians are deceived. Have not men been buried alive? Tom's father at this moment might be restored to life, if we only knew how to act."

"Then—" she said, with horrified eyes, and stopped.

He saw what he had done.

"God forgive me! No, no, not that, Mary! It's all madness and moonshine! This is delirium; it will kill me! Don't think I believe them, any more than Mannering did, or Henry did. Henry has seen much death; he could not have been deceived. Tom was dead, and your heart told you he was dead. One cannot truly make any mistake in the presence of death; I know that."

Mary was marvellously restrained, despite the fact that she had received this appalling blow and vividly suffered all that it implied.

"I will try to put it out of my mind, father," she said quietly. "But if Mr. Hardcastle is alive, I shall go mad!"

"He is not. Mannering was positive."

"Nevertheless, he may be. And if he is, then Mr. May probably is."

"Grotesque, horrible, worse than death even! Keep your mind away from it, my darling, for the love of God!"

"Who knows what we can suffer till we are called to find out? No, I shall not go mad. But I must know to-day. I cannot eat or sleep until I know. I shall not live long if they don't tell me quickly."

Her father trembled and grew very white.

"This is the worst of all," he said. "These things will leave a burning brand. I am ruined by them, and my life thrown down. I, that thought I was strong, prove so weak that I can forget my own daughter, and out of cowardly misery speak of a thing she should never have known. You have your revenge, Mary, for I shall go a broken man from this hour. Nothing can ever be the same again. My self-respect is gone. I could have endured everything else—the things that I dreaded. All I could have suffered and survived; but to have forgotten and stabbed you—"

"Don't, don't—come—we have got each other, father—we have still got each other. The dead understand everything. Who else matters? Go to your room, and let your dear mind rest. I am not suffering. We cannot alter the past, and who would wish it, if they believe in eternal life? I would not call Tom back if I had the power to do so. Be sure of that."

She spoke comfortable words to him, and supported him to his room. She knew the police would soon arrive, and though they could not report concerning the life, or death, of Peter Hardcastle, she doubted not that definite information relating to him must come to Chadlands quickly. Upon that another life might hang. Yet, when the medical man arrived from Newton, he could only say that Septimus May was dead. He was a friend of Mannering, and knew the London opinion, that this form of apparent death might in reality conceal latent possibilities of resuscitation; but he spoke with absolute certainty. He was old, and had nearly fifty years of professional experience behind him.

"The man is dead, or I never saw death," he declared. "By a hundred independent evidences we can be positive. Post-mortem stains have already appeared, and were they ever known on a living body? Of the others who died in this room I know nothing personally; but here is death, and in twenty-four hours the fact will be plain to the perception of an idiot. What has happened is this: the London police have heard of a famous, recent German case mentioned in 'Deutsche Medizinische Wochenschraft'—an astonishing thing. A woman, who had taken morphine and barbital, was found apparently dead after a night's exposure in some lonely spot. There were no reflexes, no pulse, no respiration or heart-beat. Yet she was alive—existing without oxygen—an impossibility as we had always supposed. Seeing no actual evidence of death, the physicians injected camphor and caffein and took other restorative steps, with the result that in an hour the woman breathed again! Twenty-four hours later she was conscious and able to speak. It is assumed that the poison and the cold night air together had paralyzed her vasomotor nerves and reduced her body to a state akin to hiber-nation, wherein physical needs are at their minimum. That case has doubtless awakened these suspicions, and having regard to them, we will keep the poor gentleman in a warm room and proceed with the classical means for restoring respiration."

The doctor was thus engaged when four men reached Chadlands after their nightly journey. They were detective offi-cers of wide reputation, and their chief—a grey-haired man with a round, amiable face and impersonal manner—listened to the events that had followed upon Peter Hardcastle's arrival and departure.

Sir Walter himself narrated the incidents, and perceiving his excitation, Inspector Frith assumed the gentlest and most forbearing attitude that he knew.

The police had come in a fighting humor. They arrived without any preconceived ideas or plan of action; but they were in bitter earnest, and knew that a great body of public opinion lay behind them. That Hardcastle, who had won such credit for his department and earned the applause of two continents, should have thus been lost, in a manner so mean and futile, exasperated not only his personal colleagues, but the larger public interested in his picturesque successes and achievements.

The new arrivals felt little doubt that their colleague was indeed dead, nor, when they heard of the last catastrophe, and presently stood by Septimus May, could they feel the most shadowy suspicion that life might be restored to him. Sir Walter found his nerve steadied on the arrival of these men. Indeed, by comparison with other trials, the ordeal before him now seemed of no complexity. He gave a clear account of events, admitted his great error, and answered all questions without any further confusion of mind.

"I am not concerned to justify my permission in the matter of Mr. May," he concluded. "I deeply deplore it, and bitterly lament the result; but my reasons for granting him leave to do what he desired I am prepared to justify when the time comes. Others also heard him speak, and though he did not convince my daughter, whose intellect is keener than my own, I honestly believed him with all my heart. It seemed to me that only so could any reasonable explanation be reached. Moreover, you have to consider his own triumphant conviction and power of argument. Rightly or wrongly, he made me feel that he was not mistaken—indeed, made me share his resolute convictions. These things I am prepared to explain if need be. But that will not matter to you. Personally I am now only too sure that both Septimus May and I were mistaken. I realize that there must exist some physical causes for these terrible things, that they are of human origin, and I hope devoutly that you will be permitted by Providence to discover them, and those responsible for them. But the peril is evidently still acute. The danger remains, and I need not ask you to recognize it."

Inspector Frith answered him, and proved more human than Sir Walter expected. He was an educated man of high standing in his business.

"We'll waste no time," he said. "Perhaps it is as well you are convinced, Sir Walter, that these things have happened inside natural laws, and don't depend on beings in some unknown fourth dimension. That is your affair, and I am very sure, as you say, that you can give good reasons for what you did at a future inquiry, though the results are so shocking. Poor Peter was taken back to London last night, you tell us, according to directions. If he's in the same case as this unfortunate gentleman, then there's not much doubt about his being dead. We must begin at the beginning, though for us, naturally, Hardcastle's operations and their failure are the most interesting facts to be dealt with. You have told us everything that happened to him. But we have not heard who found him."

"My nephew, Henry Lennox."

"He found Captain May, too?"

"He did. He was the last to see him alive, and the first to see him afterwards."

"Is he here?"

"He will be here in the course of the day. He travelled to London last night with the body of Mr. Hardcastle."

"Why?"

"The doctor, Mr. Mannering, wished him to do so. He desired to have a companion."

"Have you anything further that you would care to tell us?"

"Only this, that I think Mr. Hardcastle, with whom I had a long conversation on his arrival, gave it as his opinion that it was not in the Grey Room we must look for an explanation. I believe he regarded his visit to the room itself as a comparatively unimportant part of the case. He was really more interested in the life of my son-in-law and his relations with other people. I think he regarded May's death as a matter which had been determined outside the Grey Room. But, if I may presume to advise you, this view of his is surely proved mistaken in the light of his own destruction and what has happened since. It is certain now that the cause of danger lies actually in the room itself, and equally certain that what killed my son-in-law also killed Mr. Hardcastle and, last night, killed the Reverend Septimus May."

"On the fact of it, yes," admitted Frith. "I think, after we have considered the situation now developed and visited the Grey Room, we shall agree that there, at any rate, we may begin the work that has brought us. You understand we rule out the possibility of any supernatural event, as Hardcastle, of course, did. While he very properly centred on the history of Captain May, and, from his point of view, did not expect to find the accident of the captain's death in this particular place would prove important, we shall now assume otherwise, and give the room, or somebody with access to it, the credit for this destruction of human life. We shall fasten on the room therefore. Our inquiry is fairly simple at the outset, simpler than poor Hardcastle's. It will lie along one of two channels, and it depends entirely upon which channel we have to proceed whether the matter is going to take much time, and possibly fail of explanation at the end, or but a short time, and be swiftly cleared up. I hope the latter."

"I shall be glad if you can explain that remark," answered Sir Walter; but Mr. Frith was not prepared immediately to do so.

"Fully when the time comes, Sir Walter; but for the moment, no—not even to you. You will understand that our work must be entirely secret, and the lines on which we proceed known only to ourselves."

"That is reasonable, for you cannot tell yet whether I, who speak to you, may not be responsible for everything. At least, command me. I only hope to Heaven you are not going to discover a great crime."

"I share your hope. That is why I speak of two channels for inquiry," answered the detective. "Needless to say, we four men shall discuss the new light thrown upon the situation very fully. At present the majority of us are inclined to believe there is no crime, and the death of Mr. May does not, to my mind, increase the likelihood of such a thing. Indeed, it supports me, I should judge, in my present opinion. What that is will appear without much delay. We'll get to our quarters now, and ask to see the Grey Room later on."

"May I inquire concerning Mr. Hardcastle? I hope he had no wife or family to mourn him."

"He was a bachelor, and lived with his mother, who keeps a shop. The intention is to examine his body this morning, and submit it to certain conclusive tests. Nobody expects much from them, but they're not going to lose half a chance. He was a great man."

"You will hear at once from London if anything transpires to help you?"

"We shall hear by noon at latest."

Sir Walter left them then, and Masters took the four to their accommodation. Their rooms were situated together in the corridor, as near the east end of it as possible. But the four were not yet of one mind, and when they met presently, and walked together in the garden for an hour, it appeared that while two of them agreed with Inspector Frith, under whom all acted, the fourth held to a contrary view, and desired to take the second of the two channels his chief had mentioned.

Thus three men believed some extraordinary concatenation of circumstances, probably mechanical in operation, was responsible for all that had happened in the Grey Room; but the fourth, a man older than Frith, and in some sort his rival for many years, held to it that the reason of these things must be sought in an active and conscious agency. He trusted in a living cause, but felt confident that it was not a sane one. He had known a case when a madman, unsuspected of madness, had operated with extraordinary skill to destroy innocent persons and escape detection, and already he was disposed to believe that among the household of Chadlands might hide such an insane criminal.

On a similar plane, it was in his personal experience that weak-minded persons, possessed with a desire to do something out of the common, had often planned and perpetrated apparent physical phenomena, and created an appearance of supernatural visitations, only exposed after great difficulty by professional research. Along such lines, therefore, this man was prepared to operate, and he believed it might be possible that a maniac, in possession of some physical secret, would be found among the inhabitants of the manor house. He did not, however, elaborate this opinion, but kept it to himself. Indeed, the human element of jealousy, so often responsible for the frustration of the worthiest human ambitions, was not absent from the minds of the four now concerned with this problem.

Each desired to solve it, and while no rivalry existed among them, save in the case of the two older men, it was certain that the eldest of the four would not lose his hold on his own theory, or be at very vital pains to stultify it. All, however, were fully conscious of the danger before them, and Frith, from the first, directed that none was to work alone, either in the Grey Room or elsewhere.

At noon a telegram arrived for Mr. Frith from Scotland Yard. It recorded the fact that Peter Hardcastle was dead, and that examination had revealed no cause for his end. The news reached Sir Walter at once, and if ever he rejoiced in the death of a fellow-creature, it was upon this occasion. It meant unspeakable relief both for him and his daughter.

The detectives began their operations after a midday meal, and having first carefully studied the Grey Room in every visible particular, they emptied it of its contents, and placed the pictures, furniture, and statuette outside in the corridor. They asked for no assistance, and desired that none should visit the scene of their labors. The apartment, empty to the walls, they examined minutely; with the help of ladders, they investigated the outer walls on the east and south side; and they probed the chimney from above and below. They searched the adjoining room—Mary's old nursery—to satisfy themselves that no communication existed, and they drove an iron rod through the walls in various directions, only to prove they were of solid stone, eighteen inches thick within and two feet thick without. There was no apartment on the other side of the chamber. It completed the eastern angle of the house front, and behind it, inside, the corridor terminated at an eastern window parallel with the Grey Room oriel, but flat and undecorated—a modern window inserted by Sir Walter's grandfather to lighten a dark corner. Not a foot of the walls they left untested, and they examined and removed a portion of the paper upon them also. Then, taking up the carpet, they broke into the flooring and skirting boards, but discovered no indication that the grime and dust of centuries had ever been disturbed. The desiccated mummy of a rat alone rewarded their scrutiny. It lay between great timbers under the planking—beams that supported the elaborate stucco roof of a dwelling-room below.

To the ceiling of the Grey Room they next turned their attention, fastened an electric wire to the nearest point, and, through a trap-door in the roof of the passage, investigated the empty space between the ceiling and the roof. Not an inch of the massive oaken struts above did they fail to scrutinize, and they made experiments with smoke and water, to learn if, at any point, so much as a pin-hole existed in the face of the stucco. But it was solid, and spread evenly to a considerable depth. They studied it, then, from inside the room, to discover nothing but the beautifully modeled surface, encrusted with successive layers of whitewash. The workmanship belonged to a time when men knew not to scamp their labors and art and craft went hand in hand. Such enthusiasms perished with the improvement of education. They died with the Guilds, and the Unions are not concerned to revive them.

The detectives had finished this examination when, at an hour in the late afternoon, Henry Lennox and Dr. Mannering returned. The authorities had been informed of the death of Septimus May, and desired that no more than the ordinary formalities should be taken, unless their representatives at Chadlands thought otherwise. But they did not. They were now convinced that no communication existed between the Grey Room and the outer world, and they declared their determination to watch in it during the coming night. As a preliminary to this course, however, they examined each piece of furniture and every picture and other object that they had removed from the room. These told them nothing, and presently they restored the chamber in every particular, re-laid and nailed the carpet, and placed each article as it had stood when they arrived. They continued to decline assistance, and made it clear that nobody was to approach the end of the corridor in which they worked. Alive to the danger, but believing that, whatever its quality, four men could hardly be simultaneously destroyed, they prepared for their vigil. Nor did they manifest any fear of what awaited them. Facts, indeed, may be stubborn things, but even facts will not upset the convictions of a lifetime. Not one of the four for an instant imagined that a supernatural explanation of the mystery existed. Their minds were open, and their wits, long trained in problems obscure and difficult, assured them that the problem was capable of solution and within the power of their wits to solve. They apprehended no discovery from the watch to be undertaken; but, at Frith's orders, they set stolidly about it, as a preliminary to the proceedings of the following day. Once proved that the murderous force was powerless against men prepared and armed against it, and the practical inquiry as to these strange deaths would be entered upon.

They came with full powers, and designed to search the house without warning on the following morning, and examine all who dwelt in it.

Sir Walter invited them to dine with him, and they did so. There were present the master of Chadlands, Dr. Mannering—who asked to spend the night there—and Henry Lennox; while Masters and Fred Caunter waited upon them. The detectives heard with interest the result of the post-mortem conducted during the morning, and related incidents in the life of Peter Hardcastle. They were all unfeignedly amazed that a man with such a record—one who had carried his life in his hand on many occasions—should have lost it thus, at noonday and without a sound of warning to his fellow-creatures. Dr. Mannering told how he had watched the medical examination, but not assisted at it. All attempts to galvanize back life failed, as the experts engaged immediately perceived they must upon viewing the corpse; and during the subsequent autopsy, when the dead man's body had been examined by chemist and microscopist, the result was barren of any pathological detail. No indication to explain his death rewarded the search. Not a clue or suspicion existed. He was healthy in every particular, and his destruction remained, so far, inexplicable to science. Hardcastle had died in a syncope, as the other victims; that was all the most learned could declare.

Impressed by these facts, the four made ready, and Lennox observed that they neither drank during their meal nor smoked after it.

At nine o'clock they began their work of the night, but invited nobody to assist them, and begged that they might not be approached until daylight on the following morning.

Dr. Mannering took it upon himself earnestly to beg they would abandon the vigil. Indeed, he argued strongly against it.

"Consider, gentlemen," he said, "you are now possibly convinced in your own minds that the source of these horrible things is to be found outside the Grey Room, and not in it. I agree with you, so far. We have reached a pitch where, in my judgment, we are justified in believing that some motiveless malignity is at work. But by going into that room, are you not giving somebody another opportunity to do what has already been done? Evil performed without motive, as you know better than I can tell you, must be the work of a maniac, and there may exist in this house, unsuspected and unguessed, a servant afflicted in this awful way. One has heard of such things."

The eldest of his listeners felt unspeakable interest in these remarks, since his own opinion inclined in the same direction. He was, however, none the less chagrined that another should thus voice his secret theory. He did not answer, but his chief replied.

"It is proved," said Frith, "that no violence overtakes those subjected to this ordeal. And I have decided that we shall not be in danger, for this reason. We shall be armed as none of the dead were. Our precautions will preclude any possibility of foul play from a material assault. And, needless to say, we contemplate no other. We are free agents, and I should not quarrel with any among us who shirked; but duty is duty, and we have all faced dangers as great as this—probably far greater. What you say is most interesting, doctor, and I agree with you, that outside the room we must look for the explanation of these murders—if murders they are. Upon that business we shall start to-morrow. Forgive me for not going into details, because we have our personal methods. They embrace the element of surprise, and, of course, prevent any conversation concerning what we are going to do until we have done it."

"Supposing you are all found dead to-morrow?" asked Dr. Mannering bluntly.

"Then we are all found dead to-morrow; and others will have the satisfaction of finding out why."

"You suspect somebody, yet can absolve nobody?"

"Exactly, Sir Walter. I said pretty much that to the pressmen, who forced themselves in this afternoon. The accursed daily Press of this country has saved the skin of more blackguards than I like to count. Keep them and the photographers away. It ought to be criminal—their interference."

"I ordered that none was to be admitted for a moment."

"It is always very hard to keep them out. They are cunning devils, and take a perverse pleasure in adding to our difficulties.

Little they care how they defeat justice if they can only get 'copy' for their infernal newspapers."

Inspector Frith spoke with some warmth; he had little for which to thank the popular Press.

Within an hour the four departed, and it was understood that they should not be disturbed until they themselves cared to reappear.

Mannering remained with Sir Walter and Lennox. He was dejected and exceedingly anxious. But the others did not share his fears. The younger, indeed, felt hopeful that definite results might presently be recorded, and he went to his bed very thankful to get there. But Sir Walter, now calm and refreshed by some hours of sleep during the afternoon, designed to keep his own vigil.

"Poor May lies in my library to-night," he said, "and I shall watch beside him. Mary also wishes to do so. It seems a proper respect to pay the dead. The inquest takes place to-morrow, and he will be buried in his parish. We must attend the funeral, Mary and I."

"If ever a man took his own life, that man did!" declared the doctor.

CHAPTER IX.

THE NIGHT WATCH

Though a room had been prepared for Dr. Mannering, he did not occupy it long. The early hours of night found him in a bad temper, and suffering from considerable exacerbation of nerves. He troubled little for himself, and still less concerning the police, for he was human, and their indifference to his advice annoyed him; but for Sir Walter he was perturbed, and did not like the arrangements that he had planned. The doctor, however, designed to go and come and keep an eye upon the old man, and he hoped that the master of Chadlands would presently sleep, if only in his study chair. For himself he suffered a somewhat unpleasant experience toward midnight, but had himself to thank for it. He rested for an hour in his bedroom, then went downstairs, to find Mary and her father sitting quietly together in the great library. They were both reading, while at the farther end, where a risen moon already frosted the lofty windows above him, lay Septimus

May in his coffin. Mary had plucked a wealth of white hothouse flowers, which stood in an old Venetian bowl at his feet.

Sir Walter was solicitous for the doctor.

"Not in bed!" he exclaimed. "This is too bad, Mannering. We shall have you ill next. You have been on your feet for countless hours and much lies before you to-morrow. Do be sensible, my dear fellow, and take some rest—even if you cannot sleep."

"There is no sleep to-night for me. Lord knows how soon I may be wanted by those fools playing with fire upstairs."

"We cannot interfere. For myself a great peace has descended upon me, now that initiative and the need for controlling and directing is taken out of my hands. I began to feel this when poor Hardcastle arrived; but that composure was sadly shattered. I am even prepared for the needful publicity now. I can face it. If I erred in the matter of this devoted priest, I shall not question the judgment of my fellow-men upon me."

"Fear nothing of that sort," answered Mannering. "Your fellow-man has no right to judge you, and the law, with all its faults, appreciates logic. Who can question your right to believe that this is a matter outside human knowledge? Your wisdom may be questioned, but not your right. Plenty would have felt the same. When the mind of man finds itself groping in the dark, you will see that, in the huge majority of cases, it falls back upon supernatural explanations for mystery. This fact has made fortunes for not a few who profit by the credulity of human nature. Faiths are founded on it. May carried too many guns for you. He honestly convinced you that his theory of his son's death was the correct theory; and I, for one, though I deplore the fact that you came to see with his eyes, and permitted him to do what he believed was his duty, yet should be the last to think your action open to judicial blame. No Christian judge, at any rate, would have the least right to question you. In a word, there is no case yet against anybody. The force responsible for these things is utterly unknown, and if ill betides the men upstairs, that is only another argument for you."

Sir Walter put down his book—a volume of pious meditations. Events had drawn him into a receptive attitude toward religion. He was surprised at Dr. Mannering.

"I never thought to hear you admit as much as that. How strangely the currents of the mind ebb and flow, Mannering. Here are you with your scepticism apparently weakening, while I feel thankfully assured, at any rate for the moment, that only a material reason accounts for these disasters."

"Why?" asked the physician.

"Because against the powers of any dark spirit Septimus May was safe. Even had he been right and his prayer had freed such a being and cast it out of my house, would the Almighty have permitted it to rend and destroy the agent of its liberation? May could not have suffered death by any conscious, supernatural means if our faith is true; but, as he himself said, when he came here after the death of his boy, he did not pretend that faith in God rendered a human being superior to the laws of matter. If, as was suggested at dinner to-day, there is somebody in this house with a mind unhinged who has discovered a secret of nature by which human life can be destroyed and leave no sign, then this dead clergyman was, of course, as powerless against such a hideous danger as any other human being."

"But surely such a theory is quite as wild as any based on supernatural assumptions? You know the occupants of this house—every one of them, Sir Walter. Mary knows them, Henry knows them. I have attended most of them at one time or another. Is there one against whom such a suspicion can be entertained?"

"Not one indeed."

"Could the war have made a difference?" asked Mary. "We know how shell shock and wounds to a poor man's head had often left him apparently sound, yet in reality weakened as to his mind."

"Yes, that is true enough. And when the unfortunate men get back into everyday life from the hospitals, or endeavor to resume their old work, the weakness appears. I have seen cases. But of all the men in Chadlands there are only three examples of any such catastrophe. I know a few in the village—none where one can speak of actual insanity, however. Here there is only Fred Caunter, who was hurt about the head on board ship, but the injury left no defect."

"Fred is certainly as sane as I am—perhaps saner," admitted Sir Walter.

"Don't think I really imagine there is anything of the kind here," added Mannering. "But if these four men are in a condition to proceed with their work to-morrow, you must expect them to make a searching examination of everybody in the house. And they may find a good number of nervous and hysterical women, if not men. It is not their province, however, to determine whether people are weak in the head, and I know, as well as you do, that none in this house had any hand in these disasters."

"Never was a family with fewer secrets than mine," declared Sir Walter.

"The morning may bring light," said Mary.

"I feel very little hope that it will," answered Mannering. "The inquiry will proceed, whatever happens to-night, and we may all have to go to London to attend it. After they have turned Chadlands and everybody in it upside down, as they surely will, then we may be called, if they arrive at no conclusion."

"I am prepared to be. I shall not leave the country, of course, until I receive permission to do so. It must be apparent to every-body that I am, of all men, if not the most involved, at least the most anxious to clear this mystery—that nobody can doubt."

"Then you must conserve your strength and be guided," said Mannering. "I do beg of you to retire now, and insist upon Mary doing the same. Nothing can be gained by the dead, and neces-sary energy is lost to the living by this irrational vigil. It is far past midnight; I beg you to retire, Sir Walter, and Mary, too. There is nothing that should keep you out of bed, and I urge you to go to it."

But the elder refused.

"Few will sleep under this roof to-night," he said. "There is a spirit of human anxiety and distress apparent, and naturally so. I will stay here with this good man. He is better company than many of the living. I feel a great peace here. The dead sustains me."

He joined Mannering, however, in an appeal to his daughter, and, satisfied that their friend would not be far off at any time, Mary presently left them. She declared herself as not anxious or nervous. She had never believed that anything but natural causes were responsible for her husband's death, and felt an assurance that morning would bring some measure, at least, of explana-tion. She went out of the room with Mannering, and, promising her to keep a close watch on her father, the doctor left Mary, lighted his pipe, and strolled to the billiard-room. Presently he patrolled the hall and pursued his own reflections. Where his thoughts bent, there his body unconsciously turned, and, forgetting the injunction of the silent men aloft—indeed, forget-ting them also for a moment—Mannering ascended the stairs and proceeded along the corridor toward the Grey Room. But he did not get far. Out of the darkness a figure rose and stopped him. The man turned an electric torch on Dr. Mannering, and recognized him. It appeared that while one detective kept guard outside, the others watched within. At the sound of voices the door of the Grey Room opened, and in the bright light that streamed from it a weird figure stood—a tall, black object with huge and flashing eyes and what looked like an elephant's trunk descending from between them. The watchers, wearing hoods and gas masks, resembled the fantastic demons of a Salvator Rosa, or Fuselli. Their chief now accosted the doctor somewhat sharply. He knew his name and received his apology, but bade him leave the corridor at once. "I must, however, search you first," said Frith. "You were wrong to come," he continued. "This is no time to distract us. Explain to-morrow, please."

The doctor, after holding up his hands and submitting to a very close scrutiny, departed and swore at his own inadvertence. He had forgotten that, in common with everybody else involved, he must bear the brunt of suspicion, and he perceived that his approach to the Grey Room, after it was clearly understood that none should on any account attempt to do so, must attract unpleasant attention to himself. And he could offer no better excuse than that he had forgotten the order. He apprehended an unpleasantness on the following day, and wondered at himself that he could have done anything so open to question. Brain fag was a poor excuse, but he had none better.

In an hour he returned to Sir Walter, hoping to find him asleep; but the master of Chadlands was still reading, and in a frame of mind very quiet and peaceful. He regretted the forgetfulness that had taken his friend into the forbidden gallery.

"I am concerned for Mary," he said. "She is only keeping up at a terrible cost of nervous power. It is more than time that she was away; but she will not go until I am able to accompany her."

"It should not be long. We must hope they will get to the

bottom of it soon, if not to-night. I am most anxious for both of you to be off."

"We design to go to Italy. She shrinks from the Riviera and longs for Florence, or some such peaceful place."

"It will be cold there."

"Cold won't hurt us."

"Shall you shut up Chadlands?"

"Impossible. It is the only home of half my elder people. But, if nothing is discovered and we are still left without an explanation, I shall seal the Grey Room—windows, door, and hearth—unless the authorities direct otherwise. I wish I could fill the place with solid stone or concrete, so that it would cease to be a room at all."

"That you can't do," answered the practical doctor. "Such a weight would bring down the ceiling beneath. But you can make it fast and block it up if the thing beats them."

"We are like the blind moving in regions unfamiliar to their touch," said Sir Walter. "I had hoped so much from the prayer of that just man. He, indeed, has gone to his reward. He is with the boy he loved better than anything on earth; but for us is left great sorrow and distress. Still, prayers continue to be answered, Mannering. I have prayed for patience, and I find myself patient. The iron has entered my soul. The horror of publicity—the morbid agony I experienced when I knew my name must be dragged through every newspaper in England—these pangs are past. My life seems to have ended in one sense, and, looking back, I cannot fail to see how little I grasped the realities of existence, how I took my easy days as a matter of course and never imagined that for me, too, extreme suffering and misery were lying in wait. Each man's own burden seems the hardest to bear, I imagine, and to me these events have shrivelled the very marrow in my bones. They scorched me, and the glare, thrown from the larger world into the privacy of my life, made me feel that I could call on the hills to cover me. But now I can endure all."

"You must not look at it so, Sir Walter. Everybody knows that you have done no wrong, and if your judgment is questioned, what is it? Only the fate every man—great or small, famous or insignificant—has to bear. You can't escape criticism in this world, any more than you can escape calumny. It is something that you can now speak so steadfastly, preserve such patience, and see so clearly, too. But, for my part, clear seeing only increases my anxiety to-night. I don't personally care a button for the welfare of those men, since they declined to take my advice; but I am human, and as I suffer with a sick patient and rejoice when he recovers, so I cannot help suffering at the thought of the risk these four are running. They sit there, I suppose, or else walk about. They wear gas masks, and carry weapons in their hands. But if we are opposed to a blind, deaf, unreasoning force, which acts unconsciously and inevitably, then the fate of ten men would be just as uncertain as the fate of one. The thing operates by day or night—that much has been proved—and, since it is probably acting automatically, as lightning or steam, how can they escape?"

"This invisible death-dealing force may be in the control of a human mind, remember."

"It is beyond the bounds of possibility, Sir Walter."

"You are a rash man to affirm anything so definite, after what you have gone through with the rest of us. Let me, in my turn, urge you to go to your rest. These things have told upon you. You are only flesh and blood, not iron, as you fancy. The men are all right so far."

"I'll get something to eat and drink," said Mannering, "and leave you in peace for a while."

"Do. You will find all you need in the dining-room. I directed

Masters to leave ample there, in case the detectives might want food."

"Shall I bring you something—a whisky, and a biscuit?"

"No, no. I need nothing."

The doctor went his way, and passed an hour with meat and drink. Then he felt an overpowering desire to sleep, but resisted it, lighted his pipe again, and, resumed his march in the hall. He listened presently at the library door, and was gratified to hear a gentle but steady snore. The sound pleased Mannering well.

He padded about once more, resolved to keep awake until the vigil was ended. Then he would go to bed and sleep. It was now past three o'clock on a still, winter night—a lull and interval between yesterday's storm and rough weather yet to come. The doctor went out of doors for a time and tramped the terrace. A waning moon had risen, and the night was mild and cloudy.

Bright light shot out like fans into the murk from the east and south windows of the Grey Room. Returning to the house, the watcher listened at the foot of the staircase, and heard the mumble of men's voices and the sound of feet. They were changing the guard, and the detective in the corridor gave up his place to one from inside. All was well so far.

Then Mannering went to the billiard-room, lolled on the settee for a time, and drowsed through another hour. For a few minutes he lost consciousness, started up to blame his weakness, and looked at his watch. But he had only slumbered for five minutes.

At six o'clock he told himself that it was morning, and went in again to Sir Walter. The old man had wakened, and was sitting in quiet reflection until daylight should outline the great window above the dead.

"The night has been one of peace," he declared. "The spirit

of poor May seemed near me, and I felt, too, as though his son were not far off, either. Is all well with the watchers?"

"I leave you to inquire, but don't go too near them. Night fades over the woods, so the day can be said to have begun."

"Doubtless the household will be stirring. I shall go and inquire, if they will permit me to do so. Oblige me by staying here a few minutes until I call my daughter. I do not want our poor friend to be alone until he leaves us."

"I will stay here for the present. But don't let Mary be called if she is sleeping, and turn in yourself for a few hours now."

"I have slept off and on."

Sir Walter left him and ascended to the corridor. Already light moved wanly in the windows.

He stood at the top of the staircase and raised his voice.

"Is all well, gentlemen?" he asked loudly; but he received no answer.

"Is all well?" he cried again.

And then from the gloom emerged Inspector Frith. He had doffed his gas mask.

Sir Walter switched on an electric light.

"Nothing, I trust, has happened?"

"Nothing whatever, Sir Walter. No sign or sound of anything out of the common can be recorded."

"Thank Heaven—thank Heaven for that!"

"Though we had exhausted the possibilities of such a thing, we none the less expected gas," explained the detective. "That seemed the only conceivable means by which life might be destroyed in that room. Therefore we wore gas masks of the latest pattern, supposed to defy any gaseous combination ever turned out of a laboratory. It is well known that new, destructive gases were discovered just before the end of the war—gases said to be infinitely more speedy and deadly than any that were employed. As to that, and whether the Government has the secret of them, I cannot say. But no gas was liberated in the Grey Room last night. Otherwise a rat in a trap and birds in a cage, which we kept by us, would have felt it. The room is pure enough."

Sir Walter followed him down the corridor, and chatted with the other men also. They had left the Grey Room and taken off their masks; they looked weary and haggard in the waxing, white light of day.

"You've done your duty, and I am beyond measure thankful that no evil has overtaken you. What can now be prepared for you in the way of food?"

They thanked him, and declared that in an hour they would be glad of breakfast. Then Sir Walter went to his own apartments, rang, and gave the needful directions. He joined Mary soon afterwards, and she shared his thanksgivings. She was already dressed, and descended immediately to Dr. Mannering.

Henry Lennox also appeared soon afterwards. He had already learned from Fred Caunter that the watchers were safely through the night.

Chadlands was the scene of another inquest, and again a coroner's jury declared that Septimus May, as his son before him, had died by the Hand of God. Later in the day the dead man was conveyed to his own parish, and two days later Sir Walter and Mary, with her cousin, attended the funeral.

Meantime, the detectives began their serious work. They proceeded with system and upon their own plan. They omitted to question not the least of the persons who dwelt at Chadlands, and inquired also privately concerning every member of the house party there assembled when Tom May died. Into the sailor's private life they also searched, and so gradually investigated every possible line of action and point of approach to his death. The cause of this they were content to disregard, arguing that if an assassin could be traced, his means of murder would then be learned; but, from the first, no sort of light illumined their activities, and nothing to be regarded as a clue could be discovered, either in Tom May's relations with the world, or in the history and character of anyone among the many who were subject for inquiry.

Concerning the house party, only Ernest Travers and his wife had met the sailor before, on the occasion of his wedding; while as to the staff at Chadlands, nothing transpired to indicate that any had ever had occasion to feel affronted by an act of his. They were, moreover, loyal to a man and woman. They furnished no peculiarities, and gave no ground for the least suspicion. The case, in Frith's opinion, was unique, because, despite the number of persons it was necessary to study and consider, in none of their relations with the family involved could there be found a shadow of unfriendly intercourse, a harbored grudge, or a suggestion of ill-feeling. The people were all simple and ingenuous. They declared and displayed nothing but regard for their employer, and many of them had succeeded their own parents in their present employment. It was a large household, very closely united by ties of tradition and affection. Henry Lennox also proved above suspicion, though his former attachment to Mary was not concealed. It needed no great student of character, however, to appreciate his transparent honesty under examination, a remark that extended to Dr. Mannering, whose incautious advent in the corridor on the night of their vigil had offended the watchers.

For three weeks they worked industriously—without vision, but to the best of their experience and intellectual powers. In the familiar phrase, they left no stone unturned; and following their report, which frankly admitted absolute failure, a small commission instituted a further inquiry on the evidence, and invited those chiefly concerned to attend it.

Sir Walter, his daughter, Henry Lennox, and Dr. Mannering were examined with sympathy and consideration. But they could offer no opinions, throw no light, and suggest no other lines of inquiry than those already pursued.

For the world the mystery died like a new star, which was blazed into fame only to retreat or diminish and disappear once more. Fresh problems and new sensations filled the newspapers, and a time at last came when, to his relief, Sir Walter could open his morning journal and find no mention of Chadlands therein. Architects examined the room a second time, and the authorities also gave permission to certain notable spiritualists to make further nocturnal and diurnal vigils therein, though no solitary watcher was permitted. Three came and passed a day and a night in the Grey Room. They were rewarded with no phenomena whatever.

The master of Chadlands was at length informed that he might leave England, but directed to set a seal on the Grey Room, and to treat it in such a manner that it should no longer be capable of entrance.

The red tape that had wound itself about the tragedy was thus unloosed at last, and the suffering pair made all haste to get away. Its owner undertook to treat the Grey Room as directed on his return from abroad, and meanwhile had both door and window boarded up with heavy timbers.

The household was long since restored to self-possession and even cheerfulness. Some felt pride in their passing publicity, and none expressed any fear of remaining. But Sir Walter guessed that few feet would tread the great corridor until a day was near for his return.

CHAPTER X.

SIGNOR VERGILIO MANNETTI.

Sir Walter persisted in his purpose and went to Florence. He believed that here Mary might find distractions and novelties to awaken interest which would come freshly into her life without the pain and poignancy of any recollection to lessen the work of peace. For himself he only desired to see her returning to content. Happiness he knew must be a condition far removed from her spirit for many days.

They stood one evening on the Piazza of Michelangelo and saw Florence, like a city of dim, red gold extended beneath them. The setting sunlight wove an enchantment over towers and roofs. It spread a veil of ineffable brightness upon the city and tinged green Arno also, where the river wound through the midst.

Sir Walter was quietly happy, because he knew that in a fort-night his friends, Ernest and Nelly Travers, would be at Florence. Mary, too, prepared to welcome them gladly, for her father's sake. He left his daughter largely undisturbed, and while they took their walks together, the old man, to whom neither music nor pictures conveyed much significance, let her wander at will, and the more readily because he found that art was beginning to exercise a precious influence over Mary's mind. There was none to guide her studies, but she pursued them with a plan of her own, and though at first the effort sometimes left her weary, yet she persisted until she began to perceive at least the immensity of the knowledge she desired to acquire.

Music soothed her mind; painting offered an interest, part sensuous, part intellectual. Perhaps she loved music best at first, since it brought a direct anodyne. In the sound of music she could bear to think of her brief love story. She even made her father come and listen presently to things that she began to value.

Their minds inevitably proceeded by different channels of thought, and while she strove resolutely to occupy herself with the new interests, and put away the agony of the past, till thinking was bearable again and a road to peace under her feet once more, Sir Walter seldom found himself passing many hours without recurrence of painful memories and a sustained longing to strip the darkness which buried them. To his forthright and simple intelligence, mystery was hateful, and the reflection that his home must for ever hold a profound and appalling mystery often thrust itself upon his thoughts, and even inclined him, in some moods, to see Chadlands no more. Yet a natural longing to return to the old environment, in which he could move with ease and comfort, gradually mastered him, and as the spring advanced he often sighed for Devonshire, yet wondered how he could do so. Then would return the gloomy history of the winter rolling over his spirit like a cloud, and the thought of going home again grew distasteful.

Mary, however, knew her father well enough, and at this

lustrous hour, while Florence stretched beneath them in its quiet, evening beauty, she declared that they must not much longer delay their return.

"Plenty of time," he said. "I am not too old to learn, I find, and a man would indeed be a great fool if he could not learn in such a place as this. But though art can never mean much to me now, your case is different, and I am thankful to know that these things will be a great addition and interest to your future life. I'm a Philistine, and shall always so remain, but I'm a repentant one. I see my mistake too late."

"It's a new world, father," she said, "and it has done a great deal for an unhappy woman—not only in taking my thoughts off myself, but in lessening my suffering, too. I do not know why, or how, but music, and these great, solemn pictures painted by dead men, all touch my thoughts of dear Tom. I seem to see that there are so many more mighty ones dead than living. And yet not dead. They live in what they have made. And Tom lives in what he made—that was my love for him and his for me. He grows nearer and dearer than ever when I hear beautiful music. I can better bear to think of him at such times, and it will always help me to remember him."

"God bless art if it does so much," he said. "We come to it as little children, and I shall always be a child and never understand, but for you the valuable message will be received. May life never turn you away from these things in years to come."

"Never! Never!" she assured him. "Art has done too much for me. I shall not try to live my life without it. Already I feel I could not."

"What have you seen to-day?" he asked.

"I was at the Pitti all the morning. I liked best Fra Bartolommeo's great altar piece and Titian's portrait of Cardinal Ippolito dei Medici. You must see him—a strange, unhappy spirit only twenty-three years old. Two years afterwards he was poisoned, and his haunted, discontented eyes closed for ever. And the 'Concert'—so wonderful, with such a hunger-starved expression in the soul of the player. And Andrea del Sarto—how gracious and noble; but Henry James says he's second-rate, because his mind was second-rate, so I suppose he is, but not to me. He never will be to me. To-morrow you must come and see some of the things I specially love. I won't bore you. I don't know enough to bore you yet. Oh, and Allori's 'Judith'—so lovely, but I wonder if Allori did justice to her? Certainly his 'Judith' could never have done what the real Judith did. And there's a landscape by Rubens—dark and old—yet it reminded me of our woods where they open out above the valley."

He devoted the next morning to Mary, and wandered among the pictures with her. He strove to share her enthusiasm, and, indeed, did so sometimes. Then occurred a little incident, so trivial that they forgot all about it within an hour, yet were reminded of it at a very startling moment now fast approaching.

They had separated, and Sir Walter's eye was caught by a portrait. But he forgot it a moment later in passing interest of a blazoned coat of arms upon the frame—a golden bull's head on a red ground. The heraldic emblem was tarnished and inconspicuous, yet the spectator felt curiously conscious that it was not unfamiliar. It seemed that he had seen it already somewhere. He challenged Mary with it presently; but she had never observed it before to her recollection.

Sir Walter enjoyed his daughter's interest, and finding that his company among the pictures added to Mary's pleasure, while his comments caused her no apparent pain, he declared his intention of seeing more.

"You must tell me what you know," he said.

"It will be the blind leading the blind, dearest," she answered, "but my delight must be in finding things I think you'll like. The truth is that neither of us knows anything about what we ought to like."

"That's a very small matter," he declared. "We must begin by learning to like pictures at all. When Ernest comes, he will want us to live in his great touring car and fly about, so we should use our present time to the best advantage. Pictures do not attract him, and he will be very much surprised to hear that I have been looking at them."

"We must interest him, too, if we can."

"That would be impossible. Ernest does not understand pictures, and music gives him no pleasure. He regards art with suspicion, as a somewhat unmanly thing."

"Poor Mr. Travers!"

"Do not pity him, Mary. His life is sufficiently full without it."

"But I've lived to find out that no life can be." In due course Ernest and Nelly arrived, and, as Sir Walter had prophesied, their pleasure consisted in long motor drives to neighboring places and scenes of interest and beauty. His daughter, in the new light that was glimmering for her, found her father's friends had shrunk a little. She could speak with them and share their interests less whole-heartedly than of old; but they set it down to her tribulation and tried to "rouse" her. Ernest Travers even lamented her new-found interests and hoped they were "only a passing phase."

"She appears to escape from reality into a world of pictures and music," he said. "You must guard against that, my dear Walter. These things can be of no permanent interest to a healthy mind."

For a fortnight they saw much of their friends, and Mary observed how her father expanded in the atmosphere of Ernest and Nelly. They understood each other so well and echoed so many similar sentiments and convictions.

Ernest entertained a poor opinion of the Italian character. He argued that a nation which depended for its prosperity on wines and silk—"and such wines"—must have too much of the feminine in it to excel. He had a shadowy idea that he understood the language, though he could not speak nor write it himself.

"We, who have been nurtured at Eton and Oxford, remember enough Latin to understand these people," he said, "for what is Italian but the emasculated tongue of ancient Rome?"

Nelly Travers committed herself to many utterances as idiotic as Ernest's, and Mary secretly wondered to find how shadowy and ridiculous such solid people showed in a strange land. They carried their ignorance and their parochial atmosphere with them as openly and unashamedly as they carried their luggage. She was not sorry to leave them, for she and her father intended to stop for a while at Como before returning home again.

Their friends were going to motor over the battlefields of France presently, and both Ernest and Nelly came to see Sir Walter and his daughter off for Milan. Mr. Travers rushed to the door of the carriage and thrust in a newspaper as the train moved.

"I have secured a copy of last week's 'Field,' Walter," he said.

They passed over the Apennines on a night when the fireflies flashed in every thicket under the starry gloom of a clear and moonless sky; and when the train stopped at little, silent stations the throb of nightingales fell upon their ears.

But circumstances prevented their visit to the Larian Lake, for at Milan letters awaited Sir Walter from home, and among them one that hastened his return. From a stranger it came, and chance willed that the writer, an Italian, had actually made the journey from Rome to London in order that he might see Sir

Walter, while all the time the master of Chadlands happened to be within half a day's travel. Now, the writer was still in London, and proposed to stop there until he should receive an answer to his communication. He wrote guardedly, and made one statement of extraordinary gravity. He was concerned with the mystery of the Grey Room, and believed that he might throw some light upon the melancholy incidents recorded concerning it.

Sir Walter hesitated for Mary's sake, but was relieved when she suggested a prompt return.

"It would be folly to delay," she said. "This means quite as much to me as to you, father, and I could not go to Como knowing there may be even the least gleam of light for us at home. Nothing can alter the past, but if it were possible to explain how and why—what an unutterable relief to us both!"

"Henry was to meet us at Menaggio."

"He will be as thankful as we are if anything comes of this. He doesn't leave England till Thursday, and can join us at Chadlands instead."

"I only live to explain these things," confessed her father. "I would give all that I have to discover reasons for the death of your dear husband. But there are terribly grave hints here. I can hardly imagine this man is justified in speaking of 'crime.' Would the word mean less to him than to us?"

"He writes perfect English. Whatever may be in store, we must face it hopefully. Such things do not happen by chance."

"He is evidently a gentleman—a man of refinement and delicate feeling. I am kindly disposed to him already. There is something chivalric and what is called 'old-fashioned' in his expressions. No young man writes like this nowadays."

The letter, which both read many times, revealed the traits that Sir Walter declared. It was written with Latin courtesy and distinction. There were also touches of humor in it, which neither he nor Mary perceived:

"*Claridge's Hotel, London. April 9.*

"*Dear Sir Walter Lennox,—In common with the rest of the world that knows England, I have recently been profoundly interested and moved at the amazing events reported as happening at Chadlands, in the County of Devon, under your roof. The circumstances were related in Italian journals with no great detail, but I read them in the 'Times' newspaper, being familiar with your language and a great lover of your country.*

"*I had already conceived the idea of communicating with you when—so small is the world in this our time—accident actually threw me into the society of one of your personal friends. At an entertainment given by the British Ambassador at Rome, a young soldier, one Colonel Vane, was able to do me some service in a crush of people, and I enjoyed the privilege of his acquaintance as the result. I would not have inflicted myself upon another generation, but he took an interest in conversing with one who knew his own language.*

He was also intelligent—for a military man. Needless to say, he made no allusion to the tragedy at Chadlands, but when he spoke of espionage in war and kindred matters, I found him familiar with the details concerning the death of the great English detective, Peter Hardcastle. I then asked him, as being myself deeply interested in the matter, whether it would be possible to get further and fuller details of the story of 'the Grey Room,' whereupon he told me, to my amazement, that he had been at Chadlands when your lamented son-in-law, Captain Thomas May, passed out of life. I then recollected Colonel Vane's name, among others mentioned in the 'Times,' as at Chadlands when the disaster occurred.

"Finding that my curiosity was not idle, Colonel Vane accepted an invitation to dinner, and I enjoyed the pleasure of entertaining him and learning many personal and intimate particulars of the event. These were imparted in confidence, and he knew that I should not abuse his trust. Indeed, I had already told him that it was my determination to communicate with you upon the strength of his narrative.

"It seems improbable that anything I can say will bear upon the case, and I may presently find that I lack the means to serve you, or throw light where all is so profoundly buried in darkness. Yet I am not sure. Small things will often lead to greater, and though the past is unhappily beyond recall, since our Maker Himself cannot undo the work of yesterday, or obliterate events embalmed in vanished time, yet there is always the future; and if we could but read the past aright, which we never can, then the future would prove less of a painful riddle than mankind generally finds it.

"If, then, I can help you to read the past, I may at least modify your anxieties in the future; and should I, by a remote chance, be right in my suspicions, it is quite imperative that I place myself at your service for the sake of mankind. In a word, a great crime has been committed, and the situation is possibly such that further capital crimes will follow it. I affirm nothing, but I conceive the agency responsible for these murders to be still active, since the police have been so completely foiled. At Chadlands there may still remain an unsleeping danger to those who follow you—a danger, indeed, to all human life, so long as it is permitted to persist. I write, of course, assuming you to be desirous of clearing this abominable mystery, both for your own satisfaction and the credit of your house. "There is but little to hope from me, and I would beg you not to feel sanguine in any way. Yet this I do believe: that if there is one man in the world to-day who holds the key of your tribulation, I am that man.

One lives in hope that one may empty the world of so great a

*horror; and to do so would give one the most active satisfaction.
But I promise nothing.*

*"If I should be on the right track, however, let me explain the
direction in which my mind is moving. Human knowledge may not
be equal to any solution, and I may fail accordingly.*

*It may even be possible that the Rev. Septimus May did not err,
and that at the cost of his life he exorcised some spirit whose operations were permitted for reasons hid in the mind of its Creator;
but, so far as I am concerned, I believe otherwise. And if I should
prove correct, it will be possible to show that all has fallen out in a
manner consonant with human reason and explicable by human
understanding. I therefore came to England, glad of the excuse to do
so, and waited upon you at your manor, only to hear, much to my
chagrin, that you were not in residence, but had gone to Florence, a
bird's journey from my own home!*

*"Now I write to the post-office at Milan, where your servant
directed me that letters should for the moment be sent. If you are
returning soon, I wait for you. If not, it may be possible to meet in
Italy. But I should prefer to think you return ere long, for I cannot
be of practical service until I have myself, with your permission,
visited your house and seen the Grey Room with my own eyes.*

*"I beg you will accept my assurances of kindly regard and
sympathy in the great sufferings you and Madame May have been
called upon to endure.*

"Until I hear from you, I remain at Claridge's Hotel in London.

*"I have the honor to be,
"Faithfully yours,
"Vergilio Mannetti."*

To this communication, albeit he felt little hope, Sir Walter
made speedy response. He declared his intention of returning

to England during the following week, after which he hoped that Signor Mannetti would visit Chadlands at any time convenient to himself. He thanked him gratefully, but feared that, since the Italian based his theory on a crime, he could not feel particularly sanguine, for the possibility of such a thing had proved non-existent.

Mary, however, looked deeper into the letter. She even suspected that the writer himself entertained a greater belief in his powers than he declared.

"One has always felt the Grey Room is somehow associated with Italy," she said. "The ceiling we know was moulded by Italians in Elizabeth's day."

"It was; but so are all the other moulded ceilings in the house as well."

"He may understand Italian workmanship, and know some similar roof that hid a secret."

"The roof cannot conceal an assassin, and he clearly believes himself on the track of a crime." Nevertheless, Sir Walter's interest increased as the hour approached for their return home. Only when that was decided did he discover how much he longed to be there. For the horror and suffering of the past were a little dimmed already; he thirsted to see his woods and meadows in their vernal dress, to hear the murmur of his river, and move again among familiar voices and familiar paths.

Chadlands welcomed them on a rare evening of May, and the very genuine joy of his people moved Sir Walter not a little. Henry Lennox was already arrived, and deeply interested to read the Italian's letter. He and Mary walked presently in the gardens and he found her changed. She spoke more slowly, laughed not at all. But she had welcomed him with affection, and been interested to learn all that he had to tell her of himself.

"I felt that it would disappoint you to be stopped at the last moment," she said, "but I knew the reason would satisfy you well enough. I feel hopeful somehow; father does not. Yet it is hope mixed with fear, for Signor Mannetti speaks of a great crime."

"A vain theory, I'm afraid. Tell me about yourself. You are well?"

"Yes, very well. You must come to Italy some day, Henry, and let me show you the wonderful things I have seen."

"I should dearly love it. I'm such a Goth. But it's only brutal laziness. I want to take up art and understand a little of what it really matters."

"You have it in you. Are you writing any more poetry?"

"Nothing worth showing you."

She exercised the old fascination; but he indulged in no hope of the future. He knew what her husband had been to Mary, despite the shortness of their union; and, rightly, he felt positive that she would never marry again.

A mournful spectacle appeared, drawn by the sound of well-known voices, and the old spaniel, Prince, crept to Mary's feet. He offered feeble homage, and she made much of him, but the dog had sunk to a shadow.

"He must be put away, poor old beggar; it's cruel to keep him alive. Only Masters said he was determined he should not go while Uncle Walter was abroad. Masters has been a mother to him."

"Tell father that; he may blame Masters for letting him linger on like this. He rather hoped, I know, that poor Prince would be painlessly destroyed, or die, before he came back."

"Masters would never have let him die unless directed to do so."

"And I'm sure father could never have written the words down and posted them. You know father."

Letters awaited the returned travellers, one from Colonel

Vane, who described his meeting with Signor Mannetti, and hoped something might come of it; and another from the stranger himself. He expressed satisfaction at his invitation, and proposed arriving at Chadlands on the following Monday, unless directions reached him to the contrary.

When the time came, Sir Walter himself went into Exeter to meet his guest and bring him back by motor-car. At first sight of the signor, his host experienced a slight shock of astonishment to mark the Italian's age. For Vergilio Mannetti was an ancient man. He had been tall, but now stooped, and, though not decrepit, yet he needed assistance, and was accompanied and attended by a middle-aged Italian. The traveller displayed a distinguished bearing. He had a brown, clean-shaved face, the skin of which appeared to have shrunk rather than wrinkled, yet no suggestion of a mummy accompanied this physical accident. His hair was still plentiful, and white as snow; his dark eyes were undimmed, and proved not only brilliant but wonderfully keen. He told them more than once, and indeed proved, that behind large glasses, that lent an owl-like expression to his face, his long sight was unimpaired. His rather round face sparkled with intelligence and humor.

He owned to eighty years, yet presented an amazing vitality and a keen interest in life and its fulness. The old man had played the looker-on at human existence, and seemed to know as much, if not more, of the game than the players. He confessed to this attitude and blamed himself for it.

"I have never done a stroke of honest work in my life," he said. "I was born with the silver spoon in my mouth. Alas, I have been amazingly lazy; it was my metier to look on. I ought, at least, to have written a book; but then all the things I wanted to say have been so exquisitely said by Count Gobineau in his immortal volumes, that I should only have been an echo. The world is too full of echoes as it is. Believe me, if I had been called to work for my living, I should have cut a respectable figure, for I have an excellent brain."

"You know England, signor?"

"When I tell you that I married an English-woman, and that both my sons have English blood in their veins, you will realize the sincerity of my devotion. My dear wife was a Somerset."

Mary May always declared that the old Italian won her heart and even awakened something akin to affection before she had known him half an hour. There was a fascination in his admixture of childish simplicity and varied knowledge. None, indeed, could resist his gracious humor and old-world courtesies. The old man could be simple and ingenuous, too; but only when it pleased him so to be; and it was not the second childishness of age, for his intellect remained keen and moved far more swiftly than any at Chadlands. But he was modest and loved a jest. The hand of time had indeed touched him, and sometimes his memory broke down and he faltered with a verbal difficulty; but this only appeared to happen when he was weary.

"The morning is my good time," he told them. "You will, I fear, find me a stupid old fellow after dinner."

Signor Mannetti proved a tremendous talker, and implicitly revealed that he belonged to the nobility of his country, and that he enjoyed the friendship of many notable men. The subject of his visit was not mentioned on the day of his arrival. He spoke only of Italy, laughed to think he had passed through Florence to seek Sir Walter in England, and then, finding his hostess a neophyte at the shrines of art, attuned himself to the subject for her benefit.

"If you found pictures answer to an unknown need within yourself, that is very well," he declared. "About music I know little; but concerning painting a great deal. And you desire to know, too, I see. The spirit is willing, but the spirit probably does not know yet what lies in front of it. You are groping—blind, childlike—without a hand to guard and an authority to guide. That is merely to waste time. When you go back to Italy, you must begin at the beginning, if you are in earnest—not at the middle. Only ignorance measures art in terms of skill, for there are no degrees in art. None has transcended Giotto, because technique and draughtsmanship are accidents of time; they lie outside the soul of the matter. Art is in fact a static thing. It changes as the face of the sea changes, from hour to hour; but it does not progress. There are great and small artists and great and small movements, as there are great and small waves, brisk breezes and terrific tempests; but all are moulded of like substance. In the one case art, in the other, the ocean, remains unchanged. I shall plan your instruction for you, if you please, and send you to the primitives first—the mighty ones who laid the foundations. I lived five years at Siena—for love of the beginnings; and you must also learn to love and reverence the beginnings, if you would understand that light in the darkness men call the Renaissance."

He broke from Mary presently, strove to interest Sir Walter, and succeeded.

"A benevolent autocracy is the ideal government, my friend— the ideal of all supreme thinkers—a Machiavelli, a Nietzsche, a Stendhal, a Gobineau. Liberty and equality are terms mutually destructive, they cannot exist together; for, given liberty, the strong instantly look to it that equality shall perish. And rightly so. Equality is a war cry for fools—a negation of nature, an abortion. The very ants know better. Doubtless you view with considerable distrust the growing spirit of democracy, or what is called by that name?"

"I do," admitted Sir Walter.

"Your monarch and mine are a little bitten by this tarantula. I am concerned for them. We must not pander to the mob's leaders, for they are not, and never have been, the many-headed thing itself. They, not the mob, are 'out to kill,' as you say. But that State will soon perish that thinks to prosper under the rule of the proletariat. Such a constitution would be opposed to natural law and, therefore, contain the seeds of its own dissolution. And its death would be inconceivably horrible; for the death of huge, coarse organisms is always horrible. Only distinguished creatures are beautiful in death, or know how to die like gentlemen."

"Who are on your side to-day, signor?" asked Henry Lennox.

"More than I know, I hope. Gobineau is my lighthouse in the storm. You must read him, if you have not done so. He was the incarnate spirit of the Renaissance. He radiated from his bosom its effulgence and shot it forth, like the light of a pharos over dark waters; he, best of all men, understood it, and, most of all men, mourned to see its bright hope and glory perish out of the earth under the unconquerable superstition of mankind and the lamentable infliction of the Jewish race. Alas! The Jews have destroyed many other things besides the Saviour of us all."

They found the Renaissance to be the favorite theme of Signor Mannetti. He returned again and again to it, and it was typical of him that he could combine assurances of being a devout Catholic with sentiments purely pagan.

"Christianity has operated in the making of many slaves and charlatans," he said. "One mourns the fact, but must be honest. It has too often scourged the only really precious members of society from the temple of life. It has cast the brave and clean and virile into outer darkness, and exalted the staple of humanity, which is never brave, or virile, and seldom really clean. A hideous wave submerges everything that matters. The proud, the beautiful—the only beings that justify the existence of mankind—will soon be on the hills with the hawks and leopards, and hunted like them—outcast, pariah, unwanted, hated."

"The spirit of christianity is socialistic, I fear," said Sir Walter. "It is one of those things I do not pretend to understand, but the modern clergy speak with a clear voice on the subject."

"Do your clergy indeed speak with a clear voice?"

"They do; and we must, of course, listen. Truth is apt to be painful. And how can we reconcile our aristocratic instincts with our faith? I ask for information and you will forgive the personality. I find myself in almost entire agreement with your noble sentiments. But, as a good Christian, ought I to be so? How do you stand with the one true faith in your heart and these opinions in your head, signor?"

The old man twinkled and a boyish smile lighted his aged countenance.

"A good question—a shrewd thrust, Sir Walter. There can be only one answer to that, my friend. With God all things are possible."

Henry laughed; his uncle was puzzled.

"You think that is no answer," continued the Italian. "But reason also must have a place in the sun, though we have to hide it in our pocket sometimes. So many great men would not extinguish their light—and had it extinguished for them. A difficult subject. Let us continue to think in compartments. It is safer so. If you are over eighty years old, you love safety. But I love joy and romance also, and is not religion almost the only joy and romance left to us? It is affirmation remember, not negation, that makes the world go round! The 'intellectuals' forget that, and they are sterile accordingly."

Signor Mannetti's wits were something too nimble for his hearers. He talked and talked—about everything but the matter in their minds—until half-past ten o'clock, when his man came after him. Thereupon he rose, like an obedient child, and wished them "Good-night."

"Stephano is my guardian angel," he said—"a being of painful punctuality. But he adds years to my life. He forgets nothing. I wish you a kind farewell until to-morrow and offer grateful thanks for your welcome. I breakfast in my room, if you please, and shall be ready at eleven o'clock to put myself at your service. Then you will be so gracious as to answer me some questions, and I shall, please God, try to help you."

CHAPTER XI.

PRINCE DJEM

The master of Chadlands was both drawn and repelled by his guest. Signor Mannetti revealed a type of mind entirely beyond the other's experience, and while he often uttered sentiments with which Sir Walter found himself in cordial agreement, he also committed himself to a great many opinions that surprised and occasionally shocked the listener. Sir Walter was also conscious that many words uttered flew above his understanding. The old Italian could juggle with English almost as perfectly as he was able to do with his own language. He had his country's mastery of the phrase, the ironies, the double meanings, half malicious, half humorous, the outlook on humanity that delights to surprise—the compliment that, on closer examination, proves really to be the reverse. Mary's father voiced his emotions when the visitor had gone to bed.

"If it didn't seem impossible," he told Henry, "I could

almost imagine that Signor Mannetti was trying to pull my leg sometimes."

"He tries, and succeeds," answered young Lennox. "He is built that way. His mind is as agile as a monkey, despite his age. He's a sly old bird; his thoughts move a thousand times faster than ours, and they're a thousand times more subtle."

"But he's very fascinating," declared Mary.

"He's a gentleman," answered Henry—"an Italian gentleman. They're different from us in their ideas of good form, that's all. Good form is largely a matter of geography—like most other manners and customs."

"I believe in him, anyway."

"So do I, Mary. I don't think he would ever have put himself to such extraordinary trouble if he hadn't felt pretty hopeful."

But Sir Walter doubted.

"He's old and his mind plays him tricks sometimes. No doubt he's immensely clever; but his cleverness belongs to the past. He has not moved with the times any more than I have."

"His eye flashes still, and you know he has claws, but, like a dear old Persian cat, he would never dream of using them."

"I think he would," answered her cousin. "He might spring on anybody—from behind."

"He is, at any rate, too old to understand democracy."

"He understands it only too well," replied Sir Walter. "Like myself, he knows that democracy is only autocracy turned inside out. Human nature isn't constructed to bear any such ideal. It might suit sheep and oxen—not men."

"He is an aristocrat, a survival, proud as a peacock under his humility, as kind-hearted as you are yourself, father."

"I rather doubt his kindness of heart," said Henry. "Latins are not kind. But I don't doubt his cleverness. One must be on one's guard against first impressions, Mary."

"No, no one mustn't, when they're so pleasant. There is nothing small or peddling about him. It was angelic of such an old man to take so much trouble."

Henry Lennox reminded them of practical considerations.

"The first thing is to get the room opened for him. He is going to see Uncle Walter at eleven o'clock, and he'll want to visit the Grey Room afterwards. If we get Chubb and a man or two from the village the first thing in the morning, they can help Caunter to open the room and have it ready for him after lunch."

Sir Walter rang and directed that workmen should be sent for at the earliest hour next day.

"I feel doubtful as to what the authorities would say, however," he told Henry, when his orders had been taken.

"What can they say, but be well pleased if the infernal thing is cleared up?"

"It is too good to be true."

"So I should think, but I share Mary's optimism. I honestly believe that Signor Mannetti knows a great deal more about the Grey Room than he has let us imagine."

"How can he possibly do that?" asked his uncle.

"Time will show; but I'm going to back him." At eleven o'clock on the following morning the visitor appeared. He walked with a gold-headed, ebony cane and dressed in a fashion of earlier days. He was alert and keen; his mind had no difficulty in concentrating on his subject. It appeared that he had all particulars at his fingers' ends, and he went back into the history of the Grey Room as far as Sir Walter was able to take him.

"We are dealing with five victims to our certain knowledge," he said, "for there is very little doubt that all must have suffered the same death and under the same circumstances."

"Four victims, signor."

"You forget your aged relative—the lady who came to spend

Christmas with your father, when you were a boy, and was found dead on the floor. Colonel Vane, however, recollected her, because you had mentioned her when telling the story of Mrs. Forrester—Nurse Forrester."

"I never associated my aged aunt with subsequent tragedies—nobody did."

"Nevertheless, it was not old age and a good dinner that ended her life. She, too, perished by an assassin."

"You still speak of crime."

"If I am not mistaken, then 'crime' is the only word."

"But, forgive me, is it imaginable that the same criminal could destroy three men last year and kill an old woman more than sixty years ago?"

"Quite possible. You do not see? Then I hope to have the privilege of showing you presently."

"It would seem, then, that the malignant thing is really undying—as poor May believed—a conscious being hidden there, but beyond our sight and knowledge?"

"No, no, my friend. Let me be frank. I have no theory that embraces either a good or evil spirit. Believe me, there are fewer things in heaven and earth than are dreamed of in our philosophy. Man has burdened his brain with an infinite deal of rubbish of his own manufacture. Much of his principle and practice is built on myths and dreams. He is a credulous creature, and insanely tenacious to tradition; but I say to you, suspect tradition at every turn, and the more ancient the tradition, the more mistrust it. We harbor a great deal too much of the savage still in us—we still carry about far more of his mental lumber and nonsense than we imagine. Intellect should simplify rather than complicate, and those to come will look back with pity to see this generation, like flies, entangled in the webs of thought their rude forefathers spun. But the eternal verities are few; a child could count them. We are, however, a great deal too fond of believing what our ancestors believed. Alas, nobody sins more in this respect than I. Let us, then, throw overboard the supernatural, once and for all, so far as the Grey Room is concerned. No ghost haunts it; no succubus or succuba is hidden there, to harry the life out of good men and women."

"It is strange that you should take almost the identical line of thought that poor Peter Hardcastle took. I hope to God you are right!"

"So far I am most certainly in the right. We can leave the other world out of our calculations."

He asked various questions, many of which did not appear to bear on the subject, but he made no suggestions as yet, and advanced no theories. He suspected that Peter Hardcastle might have arrived at a conclusion had not death cut short his inquiry. From time to time he lifted his hand gently for silence, and permitted a reply to penetrate his mind.

"I think very slowly about new things now," he said. "An idea must sink in gradually and find its place. That is the worst of new ideas. There is so little room for them when you are eighty. The old and settled opinions fill the space, and are jealous and resent newcomers."

Sir Walter explained to him presently that the room was being opened, and would be ready after luncheon. Whereupon he expressed concern for the workers.

"Let them have a care," he said, "for, if I am right, the danger is still present. Let them work with despatch, and not loiter about."

"No harm has ever undertaken more than one, when in the room alone. The detectives saw and felt nothing."

"Nevertheless, the assassin was quite equal to smudging out the detectives, believe me, Sir Walter."

The day was fine, and Signor Mannetti expressed a wish to

take the air. They walked on the terrace presently, and Mary joined them. He asked for her arm, and she gave it.

Prince padded beside her, and the visitor declared interest in him.

"Like myself, your dog is on the verge of better things," he said. "He will do good deeds in the happy hunting grounds, be sure."

They told him the feats of Prince, and he appeared to be interested.

"Nevertheless, the faithful creature ought to die now. He is blind and paralysis is crippling his hinder parts."

Sir Walter patted the head of his ancient favorite.

"He dies on Friday," he said. "The vet will come then. I assure you the thought gives me very genuine pain."

"He has earned euthanasia, surely. What is that fine tree with great white flowers? I have seen the like before, but am sadly ignorant of horticulture."

"A tulip-tree," said Mary. "It's supposed to be the finest in Devonshire."

"A beautiful object. But all is beautiful here. An English spring can be divine. I shall ask you to drive me to primroses presently. Those are azaleas—that bank of living fire—superb!"

He praised the scene, and spoke about the formal gardens of Italy.

Then, when luncheon was finished and he had smoked a couple of cigarettes, Signor Mannetti rose, bowed to Sir Walter, and said:

"Now, if you please."

They accompanied and watched him silently, while his eyes wandered round the Grey Room.

The place was unchanged, and the dancing cherubs on the great chairs seemed to welcome daylight after their long darkness.

The visitor wandered slowly from end to end of the chamber,

nodded to himself, and became animated. Then he checked his gathering excitement, and presently spoke.

"I think I am going to help you, Sir Walter," he said.

"That is great and good news, signor."

Then the old man became inconsequent, and turned from the room to the contents. If, indeed, he had found a clue, he appeared in no haste to pursue it. He entered now upon a disquisition concerning the furniture, and they listened patiently, for he had showed that any interruption troubled him. But it seemed that he enjoyed putting a strain upon their impatience.

"Beautiful pieces," he said, "but not Spanish, as you led me to suppose. Spanish chestnut wood, but nothing else Spanish about them. They are of the Italian Renaissance, and it is most seemly that Italian craftsmanship of such high order should repose here, under an Italian ceiling. Strange to say, my sleeping apartment at Rome closely resembles this room. I live in a villa that dates from the fifteenth century, and belonged to the Colonna. My chests are more superb than these; but your suite—the bed and chairs—I confess are better than mine. There is, however, a reason for that. Let us examine them for the sake of Mrs. May. Are these carved chairs, with their reliefs of dancing putti, familiar to her—the figures, I mean?"

Mary shook her head.

"Then it is certain that in your Italian wanderings you did not go to Prato. These groups of children dancing and blowing horns are very cleverly copied from Donatello's famous pulpit in the duomo. The design is carried on from the chairs to the footboard of the bed; but in their midst upon the footboard is let in this oval, easel-picture, painted on wood. It is faded, and the garlands have withered in so many hundred years, as well they might; but I can feel the dead color quite well, and I also know who painted it."

"Is it possible, signor—this faint ghost of a picture?"

"There exists no doubt at all. You see a little Pinturicchio. Note the gay bands of variegated patterns, the arabesques and fruits. Their hues have vanished, but their forms and certain mannerisms of the master are unmistakable. These dainty decorations were the sign manual of such quattrocento painters as Gozzoli and Pinturicchio; and to these men he, for whom these works of art were created, assigned the painting and adornment of the Vatican. We will come to him directly. It was for Michelangelo to make the creations of these artists mere colored bubbles and froth, when seen against the immensity and intellectual grandeur of his future masterpieces in the Sistine. But that was afterwards. We are concerned with the Pope for whom these chairs and this bed were made. Yes, a Pope, my friends—no less a personage than Alexander VI.!"

He waited, like a skilled actor, for the tremendous sensation he expected and deserved. But it did not come. Unhappily for Signor Mannetti's great moment, his words conveyed no particular impression to anybody.

Sir Walter asked politely:

"And was he a good, or a bad Pope? I fear many of those gentlemen had little to their credit."

But the signor felt the failure of his great climax. At first he regretted it, and a wave of annoyance, even contempt, passed unseen through his mind; then he was glad that the secret should be hidden for another four-and-twenty hours, to gain immensely in dramatic sensation by delay. Already he was planning the future, and designing wonderful histrionics. He could not be positive that he was right; though now the old man felt very little doubt.

He did not answer Sir Walter's question, but asked one himself.

"The detectives examined this apartment with meticulous care, you say?"

"They did indeed."

"And yet what can care and zeal do; what can the most conscientious student achieve if his activities are confounded by ignorance? The amazing thing to me is that nobody should have had the necessary information to lead them at least in the right direction. And yet I run on too fast. After all, who shall be blamed, for it is, of course, the Grey Room and nothing but the Grey Room we are concerned with. Am I right? The Grey Room has the evil fame?"

"Certainly it has."

"And yet a little knowledge of a few peculiar facts—a pinch of history—yet, once again, who shall be blamed? Who can be fairly asked to possess that pinch of history which means so much in this room?"

"How could history have helped us, signor?" asked Henry Lennox.

"I shall tell you. But history is always helpful. There is history everywhere around us—not only here, but in every other department of this noble house. Take these chairs. By the accident of training, I read in them a whole chapter of the beginnings of the Renaissance; to you they are only old furniture. You thought them Spanish because they were bought in Spain—at Valencia, as a matter of fact. You did not know that, Sir Walter; but your grandfather purchased them there—to the despair and envy of another collector. Yes, these chairs have speaking faces to me, just as the ceiling over them has a speaking face also. It, too, is copied. History, in fact, breathes its very essence in this home. If I knew more history than I do, then other beautiful things would talk to me as freely as these chairs—and as freely as the trophies of the chase and the tiger skins below no doubt talk to Sir Walter. But are we not all historical—men, women, even children? To exist is to take your place in history, though, as in my case, the fact will not be recorded save in the 'Chronicles' of the everlasting. Yes, I am ancient history now, and go far back, before Italy was a united kingdom. Much entertaining information will be lost for ever when I die. Believe me, while the new generation is crying forth the new knowledge and glorying in its genius, we of the old guard are sinking into our graves and taking the old knowledge with us. Yet they only rediscover for themselves what we know. Human life is the snake with its tail in its mouth—Nietzsche's eternal recurrence and the commonplaces of our forefathers are echoed on the lips of our children as great discoveries."

Henry Lennox ventured to bring him back to the point.

"What knowledge—what particular branch of information should a man possess, signor, to find out what you have found?"

"Merely an adornment, my young friend, a side branch of withered learning, not cultivated, I fear, by your Scotland Yard. Yet I have known country gentlemen to be skilled in it. The practice of heraldry. I marked your arms on your Italian gates. I must look at those gates again—they are not very good, I fear. But the arms—a chevron between three lions—a fine coat, yet probably not so ancient as the gates."

"It was such a thing as bothered me in Florence," said Sir Walter. "I'd seen it before somewhere, but where I know not—a bull's head of gold on a red field."

Signor Mannetti started and laughed.

"Ha-ha! We will come to the golden bull presently, Sir Walter. You shall meet him, I promise you!"

Then he broke off and patted his forehead.

"But I go too quickly—far too quickly indeed. I must rest my poor brain now, or it will rattle in my head like a dry walnut.

When it begins to rattle, I know that I have done enough for the present. May I walk in the garden again—not alone, but with your companionship?"

"Of course, unless you would like to retire and rest for a while."

"Presently I shall do so. And please permit nobody to enter the Grey Room but myself. Not a soul must go or come without me."

Sir Walter spoke.

"You still believe the peril is material then—an active, physical thing, controlled by a conscious human intelligence?"

"If I am right, it certainly is active enough."

They went into the garden, and Signor Mannetti, finding a snug seat in the sun, decided to stop there. Henry and his uncle exchanged glances, and the latter found his faith weakening, for the Italian's mind appeared to wander. He became more and more irrelevant, as it seemed. He spoke again of the old dog who was at his master's feet.

"Euthanasia for the aged. Why not? For that matter, I have considered it for myself in dark moments. Have you ever wondered why we destroy our pets, for love of them, yet suffer our fellow creatures to exist and endure to the very dregs Nature's most fiendish methods of dissolution? Again one of those terrible problems where mercy and religion cannot see eye to eye."

They uttered appropriate sentiments, and again the old man changed the subject and broke new ground.

"There was a prince—not your old dog—but a royal lad of the East—Prince Djem, the brother of the Sultan Bajazet. Do you know that story? Possibly not—it is unimportant enough, and to this day the sequel of the incident is buried in a mystery as profound as that of the Grey Room. Our later historians whitewash Alexander VI. concerning the matter of Prince Djem; but then it is so much the habit of later historians to whitewash everybody. A noble quality in human nature perhaps—to try and see the best, even while one can only do so by ignoring the worst. Certainly, as your poet says, 'Distance makes the heart grow fonder'; or, at any rate, softer. There is a tendency to side with the angels where we are dealing with historic dead. Nero, Caligula, Calvin, Alva, Napoleon, Torquemada—all these monsters and portents, and a thousand such blood-bespattered figures are growing whiter as they grow fainter. They will have wings and haloes presently. Yet not for me. I am a good hater, my friends. But Prince Djem—I wander so. You should be more severe with me and keep me to my point. Sultan Bajazet wanted his younger brother out of the way, and he paid the Papacy forty thousand ducats a year to keep the young fellow a prisoner in Italy. It was a gilded captivity and doubtless the dissolute Oriental enjoyed himself quite as well at Rome as he would have done in Constantinople. But after Alexander had achieved the triple tiara, Bajazet refused to pay his forty thousand ducats any longer. The Pope, therefore, wrote strongly to the Sultan, telling him that the King of France designed to seize Prince Djem and go to war on his account against the Turks. This does not weary you?"

"No, indeed," declared Mary.

"Alexander added, that to enable him to resist the French and spare Bajazet's realms the threatened invasion, a sum of forty thousand ducats must be immediately forthcoming. The Sultan, doubtless appalled by such a threat, despatched the money with a private letter. He was as great a diplomat as the Pope himself, and saw a way to evade this gigantic annual impost by compounding on the death of Djem. Unfortunately for him, however, both the papal envoy and Bajazet's own messenger were captured upon their return journey by the brother of Cardinal della Rovere—Alexander's bitterest enemy. Thus the contents of the secret letter became known, and the Christian world heard with horror how Bajazet had offered the occupant of St. Peter's throne three hundred thousand ducats to assassinate Prince Djem!

"Time passed, and the Pope triumphed over his enemies. He prepared to abandon the person of the young Turk to Charles of France, and effectively checkmated the formidable Rovere for a season. But then, as we know, Prince Djem suddenly perished, and while latest writers declare that he actually reached France, only to die there, ruined by his own debaucheries, I, for one, have not accepted that story. He never reached France, my friends, for be sure Alexander VI. was not the man to let any human life stand between his treasury and three hundred thousand ducats."

Signor Mannetti preserved silence for a time, then he returned in very surprising fashion to the subject that had brought him to Chadlands. He had been reflecting and now proceeded with his thoughts aloud.

"You must, however, restrain your natural impatience a little longer, until another night has passed. I will, if you please, myself spend some hours in the Grey Room after dark, and learn what the medieval spirits have to tell me. Shall I see the wraith of Prince Djem, think you? Or the ghost of Pinturicchio hovering round his little picture? Or those bygone, cunning workers in plaster who built the ceiling? They will at least talk the language of Tuscany, and I shall be at home among them."

Sir Walter protested.

"That, indeed, is the last thing I could permit, signor," he said.

"That is the first thing that must happen, nevertheless," replied the old gentleman calmly. "You need not fear for me, Sir Walter. I jest about the spirits. There are no spirits in the Grey Room, or, if there are, they are not such as can quarrel with you, or me. There is, however, something much worse than any spirit lurking in the heart of your house—a potent, sleepless, fiendish thing; and far from wondering at all that has happened, I only marvel that worse did not befall. But I have the magic talisman, the 'open sesame.' I am safe enough even if I am mistaken. Though my fires are burning low, it will take more than your Grey Room to extinguish them. I hold the clue of the labyrinth, and shall pass safely in and out again. To-morrow I can tell you if I am right."

"I confess that any such plan is most disagreeable to me. I have been specially directed by the authorities to allow no man to make further experiments alone."

Vergilio Mannetti showed a trace of testiness. "Forgive me, but your mind moves without its usual agility, my friend. Have I not told you everything? What matters Scotland Yard, seeing that it is entirely in the dark, while I have the light? Let them hear that they are bats and owls, and that one old man has outwitted the pack of them!"

"You have, as you say, told us much, my dear signor, and much that you have said is deeply interesting. In your mind it may be that these various facts are related, and bring you to some sort of conclusion bearing on the Grey Room; but for us it is not so. These statements leave us where they find us; they hang on nothing, not even upon one another in our ears. I speak plainly, since this is a matter for plain speaking. It is natural that you should not feel as we feel; but I need not remind you that what to you is merely an extraordinary mystery, to us is much more. You have imagination, however, far more than I have, and can guess, without being told, the awful suffering the past has brought to my daughter and myself."

"Our slow English brains cannot flash our thoughts along so quickly as yours, signor," said Mary. "It is stupid of us, but—"

"I stand corrected," answered the other instantly. He rose from his seat, and bowed to them with his hand on his heart.

"I am a withered old fool, and not quick at all. Forgive me. But thus it stands. Since you did not guess, through pardonable ignorance of a certain fact, then, for the pleasure of absolute proof, I withhold my discovery a little longer. There is drama here, but we must be skilled dramatists and not spoil our climax, or anticipate it. To-morrow it shall be—perhaps even to-night. You are not going to be kept long in suspense. Nor will I go alone and disobey Scotland Yard. Your aged pet—this spaniel dog—shall join me. Good Prince and I will retire early and, if you so desire it, we shall be very willing to welcome you in the Grey Room—say some six or seven hours later. I do not sleep there, but merely sustain a vigil, as all the others did. But it will be briefer than theirs. You will oblige me?"

Mary spoke, seeing the pain on her father's face. She felt certain that the old man knew perfectly what he was talking about. She had spoken aside to Henry, and he agreed with her. Mannetti had solved the mystery; he had even enabled them to solve it; but now, perhaps to punish them for their stupidity, he was deliberately withholding the key, half from love of effect, half in a spirit of mischief. He was planning something theatrical. He saw himself at the centre of the stage in this tragic drama, and it was not unnatural that he should desire to figure there effectively after taking so much trouble. Thus, while Sir Walter still opposed, he was surprised to hear Mary plead on the visitor's behalf, and his nephew support her.

"Signor Mannetti is quite right, father; I am positive of it," she said. "He is right; and because he is right, he is safe."

"Admirably put!" cried the Italian. "There you have the situation in a nutshell, my friends. Trust a clever woman's intuition. I am indeed right. Never was consciousness of right so impressed upon my mind—prone as I am always to doubt my own conclusions. I am, in fact, right because I cannot be wrong. Trust me. My own safety is absolutely assured, for we are concerned with the operations of men like ourselves—at least, I hope very different from ourselves, but men, nevertheless. It was your fate to revive this horror; it shall be my privilege to banish it out of the earth. At a breath the cunning of the ungodly shall be brought to nought. And not before it is time. But the mills of God grind slowly. Our achievement will certainly resound to the corners of the civilized world."

"I'm as positive as the signor himself that he is safe, uncle," said Henry Lennox.

"Let us go to tea," replied Sir Walter. "These things are far too deep for a plain man. I only ask you to consider all this must mean to me who am the master of Chadlands and responsible to the authorities. Reflect if ill overtook you."

"It is impossible that it can."

"So others believed. And where are they? Further trouble would unhinge my mind, signor."

"You have endured enough to make you speak so strongly, and your brave girl also. But fear nothing whatever. I am far too deeply concerned and committed on your behalf to add a drop to the bitter drink of the past, my dear Sir Walter. I am as safe in that room as I should be at the altar steps of St. Peter's. Trust old Prince, if you cannot trust me. I rely largely on your blind pet to aid me. He has good work to do yet, faithful fellow."

"The detectives took animals into the room, but they were not hurt," said Lennox.

"Neither shall the dog be hurt."

He patted the sleeping spaniel, and they rose and went into the house together.

Mannetti evidently assumed that his wishes were to be granted.

"I will go and sleep awhile," he said. "Until an early dinner, excuse me, and let Mrs. May and Mr. Lennox convince you, as they are themselves convinced. These events have immensely excited my vitality. I little guessed that, at the end of my days, a sensation so remarkable lay in store for me. I must conserve my strength for to-night. I am well—very well—and supported by the consciousness of coming triumph. Such an achievement would have rewarded my long journey and these exertions, even had not your acquaintance been ample reward already. I will, then, sleep until dinner-time, and so be replenished to play my part in a wonderful though melancholy romance. Let us dine at seven, if you please."

His excitement and natural levity strove with the gloomy facts. He resembled a mourner at a funeral who experiences pleasant rather than painful emotions but continually reminds himself to behave in a manner appropriate to the occasion.

They sent for his man, and, on Stephano's arm, the old gentleman withdrew.

He returned for a moment, however, and spoke again.

"You will do exactly as I wish and allow no human being to enter the Grey Room. Keep the key in your pocket, Sir Walter; and do not go there yourself either. It is still a trap of death for everybody else in the world but myself."

CHAPTER XII.

THE GOLDEN BULL

When Masters came to clear the tea, he found Sir Walter still unconvinced.

"What do you think of Signor Mannetti, Masters?" asked Henry; and the butler, who was a great reader of the newspapers, made answer.

"I think he's a bit of a freak, Mr. Henry. They tell me that old people can have a slice of monkey slipped into 'em nowadays—to keep 'em going and make 'em young and lively again. Well, I should say the gentleman had a whole monkey popped in somewhere. I never see such another. He's got a tongue like a rat-trap, and he leaves you guessing every time. He's amazing clever; so's his man. That Stephano knows a thing or two! He's got round Jane Bond something disgraceful. I never knew what was in Jane—and her five and fifty if she's an hour."

"Would he be safe in the Grey Room?" said Sir Walter.

"He'd be safe anywhere. The question in my mind is whether our silver's safe; and a few other things. I catched him poking about in the silver table only this morning. He knows what's what. He knows everything. I wouldn't say he ain't one of the swell mob myself—made up to look like an old man. I'll swear he's never seen eighty years for all he pretends."

Henry laughed.

"Don't you be frightened of him, Masters; he's all right."

"Let him go in the Grey Room by all means, Mr. Henry. He knows he's safe anywhere. Yes, Sir Walter, he knows he's safe enough. He's got the measure of it."

"Prince is to go with him, Masters."

"Prince! Why, ma'am?"

"We don't know. He wishes it. He can't hurt poor old Prince anyway."

"Well, I sha'n't sleep no worse; and I hope none of you won't, if you'll excuse me. Come what will, there's nothing in the Grey Room will catch that man napping. Not that I'm against the gentleman in general, you understand. Only I wouldn't trust him a foot. He's play-acting, and he's no more a foreigner than I am—else he couldn't talk so fine English as I do, if not finer."

"Masters is on our side, father," said Mary. "And he's right. The signor is play-acting. He loves to be in the centre of the stage. All old people do, and one of the pathetic things in life is that they're seldom allowed to be. So he's making the most of his opportunity."

"And if you refuse, Uncle Walter, he'll only go away and say he cannot help you, and accuse us of giving him all this trouble for nothing," added Henry Lennox.

They had their wish at last, and when Signor Mannetti came down to an early dinner in splendid spirits, Sir Walter conceded his desire.

"Good, my friend! And do not fear that a night of anxiety awaits you. Indeed, if I am not mistaken, it will be possible for us all to sleep very soundly, though we may go to bed rather late. But I think we must be prepared not to retire till after two o'clock. I will enter upon my watch at eight—in half an hour. The door shall be left open, as you wish. But I beg that none will approach the east end of the corridor. That is only fair. I will, however, permit Mr. Lennox to station himself on the top of the great staircase, and from time to time he may challenge me. He shall say 'Is all well?' and be sure I shall answer 'All is well.' Could anything be more satisfactory?"

Signor Mannetti ate sparingly, then he donned a big, fur, motor-coat and declared himself ready. They thought he had forgotten Prince, but he insisted upon the company of the ancient spaniel. The dog had fed, and he could sleep as well in one place as another.

"Fear not," said the Italian. "I shall be considerate to your ancient pet. I do not beg his aid without reason. He is on my side and will help me if he can—infirm though he be. I have made friends with him. Set him at my feet. I will sit here under the electric light and read my Italian papers."

Thus once again a solitary occupied the Grey Room and measured his intelligence against the terrible forces therein concealed. Signor Mannetti took leave of them cheerfully at eight o'clock, and while Sir Walter and Mary descended to the library, Henry took up his station at the head of the staircase. The corridor was lighted and the door of the Grey Room left open.

But in ten minutes the watcher looked out and cried to Lennox, who sat smoking about thirty-five yards from him.

"There is a great draught here," he said. "I will close the door, but leave it ajar that we may salute each other from time to time."

The hours crept on and since everybody at Chadlands knew what was happening, few retired to rest. It was understood that some time after midnight Signor Mannetti hoped to declare the result of his experiment.

Henry Lennox challenged half-hourly, always receiving a brisk reply. But a little after half-past one his "All well, signor?" received no response. He raised his voice, but still no answer came. He went to the door, therefore, and looked into the Grey Room. The watcher had slipped down in the armchair they had set for him under the electric light, and was lying motionless, but in an easy position. He still wore his fur-coat. Prince Henry did not see. The room was silent and cold. The electric light burned brightly, and both windows were open. Young Lennox hastened downstairs. His thoughts concentrated on his uncle, and his desire was to spare him any needless shock. For a moment he believed that Signor Mannetti had succumbed in the Grey Room, as others before him, but he could not be certain. A bare half-hour had elapsed since the watcher had uttered a cheerful answer to the last summons, and told them his vigil was nearly ended. Lennox sought Masters, therefore, told him that the worst was to be feared, yet explained that the old man who had watched in the Grey Room might not be dead but sunk in sleep.

Masters was sanguine that it might be so.

"Be sure he is so. I'll fetch the liqueur brandy," and, armed with his panacea, he followed Henry upstairs. Signor Mannetti had not moved, but as they approached him, to their infinite relief he did so, opened his eyes, stared wildly about him, and then realized the situation.

"Alas! Now I have frightened you out of your senses," he said, looking at their anxious faces. "All is well. In less than another hour I should have summoned Sir Walter. But just that last half-hour overcame me, and I sank into sleep. What is the time?"

"A quarter to two, signor."

"Good! Then let your uncle be summoned. I have found out the secret."

"A thimbleful of old cognac, signor?" asked Masters.

"Willingly, my friend, willingly. I see how wise you both were. I approve and thank you. You thought that I had followed the others into the shades, yet meant to restore me if you could without frightening Sir Walter. To go to sleep was unpardonable."

Abraham Masters and Henry descended with the good news, while the old man drank.

"I shall detain you half an hour or so," he said, when they all returned to him. "But I have no fear that anybody will want to fall asleep."

Sir Walter spoke.

"Thank Heaven, signor, thank Heaven! All is well with you?"

"All is absolutely well with me, but then I have slept refreshingly for some time. You, I fear, have not closed your eyes."

"Would you have any objection to Masters hearing what you may have to tell us? By so doing a true and ungarbled report will get out to Chadlands."

"My report will go out to the whole world, Sir Walter. All is accomplished and established on certain proofs. Your good spaniel has played his part also. I salute him—the old Prince."

Henry now observed that the dog was stretched on the floor at Signor Mannetti's feet.

"Still asleep?"

Mary knelt to pat the spaniel and started back.

"How horribly cold he is!"

"For ever asleep—a martyr to science. He was to die on Friday, remember. He has received euthanasia a little sooner, and nothing in his life has become him like the leaving of it. The last victim of the Grey Room. Mourn him not, he passed without a pang—as did his betters."

"But, but—you spoke of crime and criminals!" gasped Sir Walter.

"And truly. Great crimes have been committed in this room and great criminals committed them. Is a crime any less a crime because the doers have mouldered in their dishonored graves for nearly five hundred years?"

"Your handling of speech is not ours, and you use words differently. The old dog did not suffer, you say? How did he come to die—in his sleep?"

"Even so. Without a sigh, the last venerable victim of this murdering shadow."

"You saw him die, and yet were safe yourself, sir?" asked Lennox.

"That is what happened. Now sit down all of you, father Abraham also, and in five minutes all will be as clear as day."

They obeyed him silently.

"Yes, a master criminal, one whose name has rung down the ages and will from to-morrow win a further resonance. Would that we could bring him to account; but he has already gone to it, if justice lies at the root of things, as all men pray, and you and I believe, Sir Walter. An interesting reflection: How many suffer, if they do not actually perish, from the sins of the dead? Not only the sins of our father are visited upon us, but, if we could trace the infliction, the crimes of countless dead men accomplished long before we were born into this suffering world. I speak in a parable, but this is literal, actual. Dead men committed these murders, and left this legacy of woe."

Signor Mannetti stroked the lifeless spaniel.

"When we were left alone I picked him up and set him on the bed. He did not waken, and I knew that he would never waken again. Now let us look at this noble bed, if you please. Here is the link, you see, without which so much that I told you

yesterday must have sounded no more than the idle chatter of
an old man. Come and use your eyes. Ah, if only people had
used their eyes sooner!"

They followed him, and he pointed to a framework of carved
wood that connected the four posts.

"What is this on the frieze running above the capitals of the
little Ionic pillars?"

"The papal crown and keys," said Mary.

"Good! Now regard the other side."

"A coat of arms—a golden bull on a red ground—why, father,
that was what puzzled you at Florence!"

"Surely it was. The thing stuck in my memory, yet I could not
remember where I had seen it before."

Signor Mannetti prepared for his effect, then made it.

"The arms of the Borgia! The arms of the Spanish Pope,
Alexander VI. of unholy memory. So all is told, and we will
soon go to bed. Having marked them this morning, you will see
how readily I was led into the heart of the secret. It only needed
some such certain sign. And everything that had happened was
consonant with this explanation. The first to suffer puzzled me;
but I solved that problem, too. You shall hear how each woman
and each man was slain. Look at this mattress upholstered
in satin—there lies the unsleeping thing that brings sleep so
quickly to others! I guessed it this morning; I proved it to-night.
At seventeen minutes past eight Prince was dead; but not until
I awoke, near two o'clock, did I dare approach him. For how did
he die? The moment the heat of his ancient body penetrated the
mattress under him, it released its awful venom. He stretched
himself, curled up again, and, as the exhalation rose, with
scarcely a tremor he passed from sleep into death. Needless to
tell you that I kept far from him, for I guessed that not until
the poor fellow was cold would the demon in the mattress sink

down and disappear, as the effret into his bottle. Then mattress and dog were alike harmless, as they are now. I gave him only five hours, for he was a small, thin beast, and the heat soon left his body."

"But, signor—"

"I shall anticipate all your objections if you will listen a little longer, dear Mrs. May. Let us sit again, and question me after I have spoken, if any doubts remain unanswered. Another liqueur, Masters."

He sipped, and preserved silence for a few moments, while none spoke. Then from his armchair he traversed the story of the Grey Room, and proved amazingly familiar with the smallest detail of it. Indeed, when at last he had finished, none could find any questions to ask. "There are two very interesting preliminary facts to note, my friends," began the signor. He beamed upon them, and enjoyed his own exposition with unconcealed gusto. "The first is that a room, already suffering from sinister traditions, and held to be haunted, should have been precisely that into which this infernal engine of destruction was introduced. Yet what more natural? You have the furniture, and, for the time being, do not know what to do with it. The house is already full of beautiful things, and these surplus treasures you store here, to be safe and out of the way, in a room which is not put to its proper use. You are not collectors or experts. Sir Walter's father did not share his father's enthusiasm, neither did Sir Walter care for old furniture. So the pieces take their place in this room, and are, more or less, forgotten.

"That is the first interesting fact, and the second seems to me to be this: that those who perished here in living memory all died at different places in the room, and so died that their deaths could not be immediately and undeviatingly traced to the bed. Hardcastle, for example, as you have related his conversation, did not associate the death of poor Captain May with that of the lady of the hospital eleven years before; and Sir Walter himself saw no reason to connect the still earlier death of his aged aunt, which took place when he was a boy, with the disaster that followed.

"Let us now examine for a moment the amazing fact that none of the stigmata of death was found in those who perished here.

"Death has three modes—the pale horseman strikes us down by asphyxia, by coma, and by syncope. In asphyxia he stabs the lungs; in coma his lance is aimed at the brain; in syncope, at the heart.

"When a man dies by asphyxia, it means that the action of the muscles by which he breathes is stopped, or the work of his lungs prevented by injury, or the free passage of air arrested, as in drowning, or strangulation. It may also mean that embolism has taken place, and the pulmonary artery is blocked, withholding blood from the lungs. But it was not thus that any died in this chamber.

"Coma occurs through an apoplexy, or concussion; by the use of certain narcotic or mineral poisons; and in various other ways, all of which are ruled out for us.

"There remains syncope. A heart ceases to beat from haemorrhage, or starvation, from exhaustion, or the depressing influence of certain drugs. They who died here died from syncope; but why? No autopsy can tell us why. They passed with only their Maker to sustain them, and none leaves behind an explanation of what overtook him, or her. Yet we know full well, even in the case of Peter Hardcastle, concerning whom the police felt doubt, that he was quite dead before Mr. Lennox discovered him and picked him up. We know that the phenomena of rigor mortis had already set in before his body reached London.

"Nothing, however, is new under the sun. Many journals

related the fact that these people had passed away without a cause, as though it were an event without a parallel. It is not. Your Dr. Templeman, in 1893, describes two examples of sudden death with absolute absence of any pathological condition in any part of the bodies to account for it. He describes the case of a man of forty-three, and calls it 'emotional inhibition of the heart.' The heart was arrested in diastole, instead of systole, as is usually the case; the mode of death was syncope; the cause of death, undiscoverable.

"A layman may be permitted, I suppose, to describe 'emotional inhibition of the heart' as 'shock'; but we know, in our cases, that if a shock, it was not a painful one—perhaps not even an unpleasant one. Since all other emotions can be pleasant or unpleasant, why must we assume that the supreme emotion of death may not be pleasant also, did we know how to make it so? Perhaps the Borgia, among their secrets, had discovered this. At least the familiar signs of death were wholly absent from the countenances of the dead. The jaws were not set; the familiar, expressions were not changed, as usually happens from rigidity of facial muscles; their faces were not sallow; their temples were not sunk; their brows were not contracted.

"We will now take the victims, one by one, and show how death happened to each of them, yet left no sign that it had happened. Frankly, the first case alone presented any difficulties to me. For a time I despaired of proving how the bed had destroyed Sir Walter's ancestor, because she had not entered it. But the difficulty becomes clear to one possessing our present knowledge, for once prove the properties of the bed, and the rest follows. You will say that they were not proved, only guessed. That was true, until Prince died. His death crowned my edifice of theory and converted it to fact. As to why the bed has these properties, that is for science to find out presently.

"To return, then, to the old lady, the ancient woman of your race, who came unexpectedly to the Christmas re-union and was put to sleep in the Grey Room at her own wish. She was found dead next morning on the floor. She had not entered the bed. The exact facts have long disappeared from human knowledge, and it is only possible to re-construct them by inference and the support of those straightforward events that followed. I conceive, then, that though the old lady did not create the warmth that liberated the evil spirit of the bed and so destroyed her, that warmth was nevertheless artificially created. What must have happened, think you? The bed is made up in haste and the fire lighted. But the fire is a long way from the bed, and would have no effect to create the necessary temperature. There is, however, a hot-water bottle in the bed, or a hot brick wrapped in flannel. The old lady is about to enter her bed. She has extinguished her candle, but the flame of the fire gives light. She has prayed; she throws off her dressing-gown and flings back the covering of the bed, to fall an instant victim to the miasma. She drops backward and is found dead next morning, by which time the bottle and bed are also cold.

"Taken alone, I grant this explanation may fail to win your sympathy; but consider the cumulative evidence in store. The old lady may, of course, have died a natural death. She may not have turned down the bed. There is nobody living to tell us. All that Sir Walter can recollect is that she was found on the floor of the room dead. Exactly where, he does not remember. But for my own part I have no doubt whatever that her death took place in that way.

"We are on safer ground with the other tragic happenings, though, save in the case of Nurse Forrester, there is nothing on the surface of events to connect their deaths with the accursed bed. You will see, however, that it is very easy to do so. In the lady's case all is clear enough. She goes to bed tired and she sleeps peacefully into death without waking. She is probably asleep within ten minutes, before her own warmth has penetrated through sheet and blanket to the mattress beneath and so destroyed her. Suppose that she is dead in half an hour. She retired to rest at ten o'clock; she is called at seven; the room is presently broken into and she is then not only dead, but cold. The demon has gone to sleep again under its lifeless burden. Now had she been stout and well covered, there had hardly been time for her to grow cold, and those who came to her assistance might even have perished, too. But she is a little, thin thing, and the heat has gone out of her. This assured the safety of those who came to the bedside. One can make no laws as to the time necessary for a dead body to grow as cold as its surroundings. The bodies of the old and the young cool more quickly than those of adult persons. If the conditions are favorable a body may cool in six to eight hours. Prince took but five, poor little bag of bones.

"In the case of Captain May the conditions are altogether different. Let me speak with all tenderness and spare you pain. Be sure that he suffered no more than the others. The bed is now no longer made; the mattress is bare. That matters not to him. Clad in his pyjamas, with a railway rug to cover him and his dressing-gown for a pillow, he flings himself down, and from his powerful and sanguine frame warmth is instantly communicated to the mattress that supports him. Probably but a few minutes were sufficient to liberate the poison. He is not asleep, but on the edge of sleep when he becomes suddenly conscious of physical sensations beyond his experience. He had breathed death, but yet he is not dead. His brain works, and can send a message to his limbs, which are still able to obey. But his hour has come. He leaps from the bed in no suffering, but conscious, perhaps of an oppression, or an unfamiliar odor—we cannot say what. We only know that he feels intense surprise, not pain for in that dying moment his emotions are fixed for ever by the muscles of his face. He needs air and seeks it. He hurries to the recess, kneels on the cushion, and throws open the window. Or the window may have been already open—we cannot tell. To reach it is his last conscious act, and in another moment he is dead. The bed is not suspected. Why should it be? Who could prove that he had even laid down upon it? Indeed it was believed and reported at the inquest that he had not done so. Yet that is what unquestionably happened. Otherwise his candle would have burned to the socket. He had blown it out and settled to rest, be sure.

"We have now to deal with the detective, and here again there was nothing to associate his death with the bed of the Borgia. Yet you will see without my aid how easily he came by his death. Peter Hardcastle desires to be alone, that he may study the Grey Room and everything in it. He is left as he wishes, walks here and there, sketches a ground plan of the room and exhausts its more obvious peculiarities. Would that he had known the meaning of the golden bull! Presently he strikes a train of thought and sits down to develop it. Or he may not have finished with the room and have taken a seat from which he could survey everything around him. He sits at the foot of the bed—there on the right side. He makes his notes, then his last thoughts enter his mind—abstract reflection on the subject of his trade. For a moment he forgets the matter immediately in hand and writes his ideas in his book. He has been sitting on the bed now for some while—how long we know not, but long enough to create the heightened temperature which is all the watchful fiend within the mattress requires to summon him. Then ascends the spirit of death, and Hardcastle, surprised as Captain May was surprised, leaps to his feet. He takes two or three steps forward; his book and pen fall from his hand and he drops upon his face—a dead man. He is, of course, still warm when Mr. Lennox finds him; but the bed he leaped from is cold again and harmless—its work done.

"There remains the priest, the Rev. Septimus May. He neither lay on the bed, nor sat upon it. But what did he do? He clearly knelt beside it a long time, engaged in prayer. Nothing more natural than that he should stretch his arms over the mattress; bury his face in his hands, and so remain in commune with the Almighty, uttering petition after petition for the being he conceived as existing in the Grey Room, without power to escape from it. Thus leaning upon the bed with his arms stretched upon it and his head perhaps sunk between them, he presently creates that heightened temperature sufficient to arouse the destroyer. It enters into him—how, we know not yet—and he sinks unconscious to the floor, while the bed is quickly cold again.

"As to the four detectives—Inspector Frith and his men—pure chance saved the life of at least one of them, and by so doing, chance also prevented them from discovering that the bed in their midst was the seat of all the trouble. Had one among them taken up his watch upon it, he would certainly have died in the presence of his collaborators; but the men sat on chairs in the corners of the room, and the chairs were harmless. Whether their gas masks would indeed have saved them remains, of course, to be proved. I doubt it.

"Such, my friends, were the masterpieces of the Borgia, for whom the profoundest chemists worked willingly enough and by doing so doubtless made their fortunes. Their poisons were so designed to act that, by their very operation, the secrets of them were concealed, and all clues obliterated. Chemistry knows nothing of the supernatural, yet can, as in this case, achieve results that may well appear to be black magic.

"And if we, of this day, fail to find them out, it is easy to guess that in their own times, much that they caused to be done was set down to the operations of Heaven alone.

"Science will be deeply interested in your Borgia mattress, Sir Walter. Science, I doubt not, will carefully unpick it and make a series of very remarkable experiments; yet I make bold to believe that science may be baffled by the cunning and forgotten knowledge of men long dust. We shall see as to that."

He rose and bade Masters call Stephano. Then, with a few words, they parted, and each shook the old man's hand and expressed a deep and genuine gratitude before they did so.

"A little remains to add," said Signor Mannetti. "You shall hear what it is to-morrow. For the moment, 'Good-night!' It has been a crowning joy to my long life that I was able to do this service to new and valued friends."

In the servants' hall next morning Masters related what he had heard.

"And if you ask me," he concluded, "I draw back what I thought about him being younger than he pretends. He's older— old as the hills—older than that horror in the Grey Boom. He's a demon; and he's killed the old dog; and I believe he's a Borge himself if the truth was known."

CHAPTER XIII.

TWO NOTES

They walked in the garden next morning, and Sir Walter delayed to write to Scotland Yard until after seeing Signor Mannetti again. The old gentleman descended to them presently, and declared himself over-fatigued.

"I must sit in the sun and go to sleep again after lunch," he said. "Stephano is annoyed with me, and hints at the doctor."

"Mannering will be here to lunch. You will understand that nobody is more deeply interested in these things than he."

"But yourself," said Mary. "Come and sit down and rest. You are looking very tired to-day."

"A little reaction—no more. It was worth it." He then proceeded where he had broken off on the preceding night.

"There remains only to tell you how I found myself caught up in your sad story. It had not occurred to you to wonder?"

"I confess I had never thought of that, signor. You made us forget such a trifling detail."

"But, none the less, you will want to know, Sir Walter. Our

215

common friend, Colonel Vane, put the first thought in my head. He laid the train to which I set the match so well. He it was who described the Grey Room very exactly, and the moment that I heard of the ancient carved furniture, I knew that he spoke of curios concerning which I already had heard. The name of Lennox completed the clue, for that had already stirred memories in my ancient mind. I had listened to my father, when I was young, telling a story in which a bed and chairs and a gentleman named Lennox were connected. He spoke of an ancient Italian suite of three pieces, the work of craftsmen at Rome in the fifteenth century. It was papal furniture of the early Renaissance, well known to him as being in a Spanish collection—a hundred and fifty years ago that is now— and when these things came into the market, he rejoiced and hurried off to Valencia, where it was to be sold. For he was even such a man as your grandfather—a connoisseur and an enthusiastic collector. But, alas, his hopes were short-lived; he found himself in opposition to a deeper purse than his own, and it was Sir John Lennox, not my father, who secured the bed and the two chairs that go with it. These things, as I tell you, returned to my recollection, and, remembering them, I guessed myself upon the right track. The arms of the Borgia, and the successful experiment with the dog, Prince, proved that I was correct in guessing where the poison lay hidden."

"It is impossible to express my sense of your amazing goodness, or my gratitude, or my admiration for your genius," declared Sir Walter; but the other contradicted him.

"Genius is a great word to which I can lay no claim. I have done nothing at all that you yourself might not have done, given the same knowledge. As for gratitude, if indeed that is not too strong an expression also, you can show gratitude in a very simple manner, dear friend. I am a practical, old man and, to be honest, I very greatly covet the Borgia bed and chairs. Now, if indeed you feel that I am not asking too grand a favor—a favor out of all keeping with my good offices on your behalf—then let me purchase the bed and chairs, and convey them with me home to Rome. It is seemly that they should return to Rome, is it not? Rome would welcome them. I much desire to sleep in that bed—to be where I am so sure Prince Djem lay when he breathed his last. Yes, believe me, he received your bed as a gracious present from Alexander VI. The Borgia were generous of such gifts."

"The bed and chairs are yours, my dear signor, and the rest of the contents of the Grey Room, also, if you esteem them in any way."

"Positively I could not, Sir Walter."

"Indeed you shall. It is done, and leaves me greatly your debtor still."

"Then be it so. I thank you from the bottom of my heart. Nor will I say that you oppress me with such extraordinary generosity, for is it not more blessed to give than receive? Heavens knows what dark evils the bed may have committed in the course of its career, but its activities are at an end. For me it shall bring no more than honest slumber. But the mattress—no. I do not want the mattress. That will be a nice present for the museum of your Royal College of Surgeons."

A week later the old man was sufficiently rested, and he returned home, taking his treasures with him. But he did not depart until he had won a promise that Sir Walter and Mary would visit him at Rome within the year.

Experts again descended upon Chadlands, packed the source of tribulation with exceeding care, and conveyed it to London for examination. Those destined to make the inquiry were much alive to their perils, and took no risk.

Six weeks later letters passed between England and Rome, and Sir Walter wrote to Signor Mannetti, sending such details as he was able to furnish.

"A thin, supple wire was found to run between the harmless flock of the mattress and the satin casing," wrote Sir Walter. "Experiments showed that neither the stuffing nor the outer case contained any harmful substance. But the wire, of which fifty miles wound over the upper and lower surfaces of the mattress under its satin upholstery, proved infinitely sensitive to heat, and gave off, or ejected at tremendous speed, an invisible, highly poisonous matter even at a lower temperature than that of a normal human being. Insects placed upon it perished in the course of a few hours, and it destroyed microscopic life and fish and frogs in water at comparatively low temperatures, that caused the living organisms no inconvenience until portions of the wire were introduced. A cat died in eight minutes; a monkey in ten. No pain or discomfort marked the operation of the wire on unconscious creatures. They sank into death as into sudden sleep, and examination revealed no physical effects whatever. The wire is an alloy, and the constituent metals have not yet been determined; but it is not an amalgam, for mercury is absent. The wire contains thallium and helium as the spectroscope shows; but its awful radioactivity and deadly emanation has yet to be explained. The chemical experts have a startling theory. They suspect there is a new element here—probably destined to occupy one of the last unfilled places of the Periodic Table, which chronicles all the elements known to science. Chemical analysis fails to reach the radio-active properties, and for their examination the electroscope and spinthariscope are needful. With these the radio-chemists are at work. The wire melted at a lower temperature than lead, but melting did not destroy its potency. After cooling, the metal retained its properties and was still responsive, as before, to warmth. But experiment shows that in a molten state, the metal of the wire increases in effect, and any living thing brought within a yard of it under this condition succumbs instantly. Its properties cannot be extracted, so far, from the actual composition of the wire. They prove also that the emanation from the warmed wire is exceedingly subtle, tenuous, and volatile. Save under conditions of super-heat, it only operates at two feet and a few inches, and the wire naturally grows cold very quickly. It is almost as light as aluminium. A gas mask does not arrest the poison; indeed, it evidently enters a body through the nearest point offered to it and a safe shield has not yet been discovered.

"I shall tell you more when we know more," concluded Sir Walter. "But at present it looks as though your prophecy were correct, and that science is not going to get at the bottom of the horrible secret easily. Dr. Mannering says that the properties of the elements have yet to be fully determined, while the subject of alloys was never suspected of containing such secrets as may prove to be the case. If more there is to learn, you shall learn it."

In his reply, Signor Mannetti declared that the Borgia bed continued to be a source of extreme satisfaction and comfort to him.

"As yet no vision has broken my slumbers, but I continue to hope that the Oriental features of Sultan Bajazet's brother may presently revisit the place of his taking off, and that Prince Djem will some night afford me the pleasure of a conversation. How much might we tell each other that neither of us knows!

"As to the wire, my friend, I will explain to you how that was probably created and, right or wrong, there is nobody on this earth at present who can prove my theory to be mistaken. Be sure that a medieval alchemist, searching in vain for elixir vitae, or the philosopher's stone, chanced upon this infernal synthesis and fusion. For him, no doubt, it proved a philosopher's stone in earnest, for the Borgia always extended a generous hand to those who could assist their damnable activities. Transmutation—so a skilled friend assures me—is now proved to be a fact, and another generation will be able perhaps to make gold, if the desire for that accursed mineral continues much longer to dominate mankind.

"Farewell for the present. Again to see you and your daughter is one of those pleasures lying in wait for me, to make next winter a season of gladness rather than dismay. But do not change your minds. One must keep faith with a man of eighty, or risk the possibilities of remorse."

OTTO PENZLER'S
LOCKED ROOM LIBRARY

FROM MYSTERIOUSPRESS.COM
AND OPEN ROAD MEDIA

  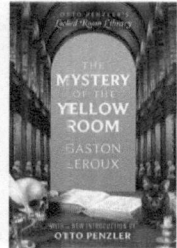

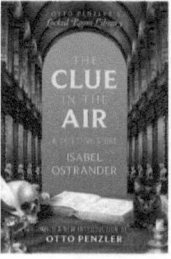 

MYSTERIOUSPRESS.COM

Otto Penzler, owner of the Mysterious Bookshop in Manhattan, founded the Mysterious Press in 1975. Penzler quickly became known for his outstanding selection of mystery, crime, and suspense books, both from his imprint and in his store. The imprint was devoted to printing the best books in these genres, using fine paper and top dust-jacket artists, as well as offering many limited, signed editions.

Now the Mysterious Press has gone digital, publishing ebooks through **MysteriousPress.com**.

MysteriousPress.com offers readers essential noir and suspense fiction, hard-boiled crime novels, and the latest thrillers from both debut authors and mystery masters. Discover classics and new voices, all from one legendary source.

FIND OUT MORE AT

WWW.MYSTERIOUSPRESS.COM

FOLLOW US:

@emysteries and Facebook.com/MysteriousPressCom

MysteriousPress.com is one of a select group of publishing partners of Open Road Integrated Media, Inc.

THE MYSTERIOUS BOOKSHOP, founded in 1979, is located in Manhattan's Tribeca neighborhood. It is the oldest and largest mystery-specialty bookstore in America.

The shop stocks the finest selection of new mystery hardcovers, paperbacks, and periodicals. It also features a superb collection of signed modern first editions, rare and collectable works, and Sherlock Holmes titles. The bookshop issues a free monthly newsletter highlighting its book clubs, new releases, events, and recently acquired books.

58 Warren Street
info@mysteriousbookshop.com
(212) 587-1011
Monday through Saturday
11:00 a.m. to 7:00 p.m.

FIND OUT MORE AT:

www.mysteriousbookshop.com

FOLLOW US:

@TheMysterious and Facebook.com/MysteriousBookshop

INTEGRATED MEDIA

Find a full list of our authors and
titles at www.openroadmedia.com

FOLLOW US
@OpenRoadMedia